William Graham

Last Links with Byron, Shelley, and Keats

William Graham

Last Links with Byron, Shelley, and Keats

ISBN/EAN: 9783337105952

Printed in Europe, USA, Canada, Australia, Japan

Cover: Foto ©Andreas Hilbeck / pixelio.de

More available books at **www.hansebooks.com**

Last Links with
Byron, Shelley, and Keats

BY

WILLIAM GRAHAM

LONDON

LEONARD SMITHERS & CO.

5 OLD BOND STREET, W.

1898

TO MY WIFE

CONTENTS

INTRODUCTION

I HAVE been asked to write an introduction to the
following articles, appearing now for the first time
in book form—an introduction rendered doubtless
to some extent necessary by the numerous contro-
versies they aroused, and the great attention they
claimed at the time of their appearance in monthly
review form. The writer may perhaps be permitted
to say without egotism that it appears to him that
a longer life than the fugitive life of the magazine
or review paper is due to articles written under
such very exceptional conditions; or rather he
should say it is due to the public that papers
throwing such a flood of new light upon the personalities of the three greatest poets of this century
should be permanently preserved in book form. He
himself is a man who, having been imbued from
childhood with a passionate love, almost idolatry,
of poetry and poets, and having in earliest youth
been granted special opportunities of conversing
with two of those who played so prominent a part
in the lives of these three great poets, and even of
forming an intimate and affectionate friendship with
one of them, is placed in a unique position in
regard to the present (indeed, almost in regard to
the immediately preceding) generation, and it would

be mere affectation for him to attempt to deny, what all the leading organs of the press stated at the time of their appearance, that these articles possess a unique literary value. The writer looks upon himself as a mere humble instrument. Possibly, indeed probably, it is rare in the history of the press that a series of review articles have created such feverish excitement as these. Leaders were allotted to them in nearly all the prominent metropolitan and provincial papers, and in many American and colonial journals. Several well-known continental journals also reviewed them at length—a most unusual compliment to be paid by critics, whether French or German, to articles of a purely literary nature in English reviews; though the attention they attracted in Italy is no doubt more easily explained, as all the three great poets of whom my articles speak, and both of my interlocutors who were the *media* of my obtaining such exceptional information as to those three mighty companions of the past who have made with refracted splendour their own names immortal too, lived in Italy—the great poets for a large part of their short lives, and the others for a proportional part of their extended lives—while all except Byron died there; indeed, almost every one connected with Byron and Shelley seems to have gravitated sooner or later to that enchanted land.

For the most part the press of all countries was most kindly, and all such reviewers I cordially thank, but certain weak-minded Shelley enthusiasts took another tack, and attacked me bitterly for what they were pleased to consider as the vilification of their idol's character. As regards Byron my joints re-

mained unwrung ; and the only two living men,
except perhaps Mr Jeaffreson, whom I consider
capable of expressing in any way an authorative
opinion on the subject—namely, Mr Kegan Paul
and Mr Murray—told me that they consider my
final article, "The Secret of the Byron Separation,"
the true and only explanation of the mystery which
has always overshadowed that mysterious breach.
But Byron has not been such a prey for the faddist
and the *fainéant* as Shelley. Byron was complex
indeed ; but his was essentially a masculine complexity. It was not the complexity of Shelley, or
rather the eccentricity of Shelley (for, with all his
genius and obscurity, the man was, to my mind,
not particularly complex) which horrified the Mrs
Grundy, if that lady were then invented, of the
early century even more than Byron, but who would
have been considered, in our larger-minded age,
almost fitted to deliver lectures in Exeter Hall, or,
at least, to write for the *Nineteenth Century*, the
review in which my own two first chaste articles
of this series appeared. Byron would have been a
mauvais sujet at any epoch, but his was the
"naughtiness" for which the world has more human
sympathy than for the dogmas and dreams of
Shelley's overwrought brain. But in those days of
the early century a hatred and distrust of all ideas
in any way connected with the French Revolution
was in the air, and the age when men could believe
what they pleased and say what they pleased provided they conformed fairly well to the usages of
society and the aforesaid Mrs Grundy, was far from
dawning, although rank profligacy was considered
very excusable, if not even an ornament to a young

xi

nobleman. Shelley's ideas, which he insisted with true propagandist zeal in ramming into the very teeth of the society of the day, brought him into far more trouble than Byron's profligacy would ever have done for him. The real original reason of the outcry against Byron was simply that the women made such a ridiculous fuss about him that the men grew jealous, and were not satisfied until he was hounded out of England.

There is, however, a clique which had made what Mr Rudyard Kipling would term "a little tin god" of Shelley; and the members of this absurd coterie, in affecting to raise their idol above ordinary human nature, really do his fame nothing but great disservice in depicting him as what that very caustic and sarcastic lady Miss Clairmont termed "an inspired idiot." Some of these good people seemed to have contracted the idea that Shelley is their exclusive property, and have attacked me furiously because in my pages he has been set before the world as a reasonable being, upon the authority of one who had the best opportunities of judging. To this I have, however, alluded in the body of this book; but as an amusing instance of what I mean by saying that some of these people would appear to consider Shelley as a personal appanage I may mention that, among endless letters from all sorts and conditions of people, which the following chapters have procured me, I received one from a rather noted Shelleyolater, who was much incensed with me for stating that the Shelleys had visited Marlow in 1815, as there was no record of a residence there before 1817. I did not think it worth while replying to the letter, but

shortly afterwards chanced to meet the same gentleman, among the weird shades of the underground
one dark winter's night. I am a naturally timid
man, and the reader may imagine my terror when
a sepulchral voice called out my name from the
corner of the carriage, half-hidden as was the figure
of the speaker in the fog and gloom. The infuriated
Shelleyan, or rather (for I yield to no one in my
admiration of Shelley, it is only to the manner of
it that I take exception) let me say, Shelleyolater,
took me roundly to task, first, for not replying to
his letter, the contents of which he repeated. I
merely replied that I presumed as he was born
some considerable time after Shelley's death he
would scarcely set up a claim to omniscience as to
the manner in which Shelley employed every day
of his life, and that although it was perfectly true
that the Shelleys did not permanently reside in
Marlow until 1817, I could certainly see no possible
object in Miss Clairmont's telling me of this expedition to look for a house there just previously
to the Geneva meeting, if such an event had never
taken place, when my irate interlocutor made himself
supremely ridiculous by the surely unprecedented objection on the part of a man who is supposed to be one
of "light and leading," or in any case of learning, by
making, I say, the extraordinary objection to Miss
Clairmont's account of her visit with Byron to the
Shelleys, and the incident of the French prisoners,
that "the idea of French prisoners being sent to
Marlow was absurd." "Why" (I again quote)
"should they be sent to Marlow?" That is a
question I cannot profess to answer; but as many
much less omniscient people than Macaulay's

"school-boy" know, French prisoners were sent to all sorts of out-of-the-way places, and particularly along the river, and that a number of them were sent to Marlow under the circumstances I (as the mouthpiece of Miss Clairmont) relate, is notorious; and to the present day the remains of the chains by which they were attached can be seen in the walls which divide the quaint old garden of "The Crown" from the stable-yard.

Tantaene animis coelestibus irae !

What utter nonsense the paltry passions of envy and jealousy can make a man talk, even one supposed to be learned; but I at least will be generous, and not mention this particular celestial's name. Oddly enough, however, I rather fancy he is a member of the Omar Khayyam Club, which even now, as I write this in the sweet scented air of this summer of summers a little farther up stream, is holding high festival — one of its periodical high festivals — at the Crown Inn. Perchance, therefore, by this time "mine enemy" has taken the opportunity *de se renseigner*—at least, let us hope so.

I may add to this, that Miss Clairmont explained to me that, on the occasion of the visit she and Byron paid to the Shelleys, at Marlow, the latter were actually living at Bishopsgate, farther down the river; but that Shelley's intimate friend, Thomas Love Peacock, who also shared the singular fate of nearly all his intimates, and lived to extreme old age, was stopping at Marlow, and constantly came over to see them; while Shelley, who was a superb walker, and devoted to the river, which gave the inspiration to some of his finest poetry, often

xiv

accompanied him, not only to Marlow, but to much more remote parts of the river. On this occasion the two were on a visit of a couple of days or so to Peacock—a kind of prospecting expedition—as he was very anxious that they should also take up their abode in that charming little town, which, as a matter of fact, they did the following year. I need not add that Peacock's name became subsequently familiar to all with more than an outside acquaintance with English literature, and that he was one of the finest classical scholars of this century—indeed his ultra-correct, classical taste even led him to the extreme of disapproving somewhat of Shelley's magnificent lyric drama, *The Prometheus Unbound.* The reason why the Shelleys did not present him to Byron is, I should say, obvious, even to the clique to which I have alluded.

Another strange complaint made by Shelleyolaters against me is that I have given it to be understood that Shelley and his sister-in-law (as I will call Miss Clairmont for the nonce) were—what shall I say? How shall I put it? My natural timidity comes in here again—well, not absolutely on such platonic terms as might be desired. I beg your pardon, my dear Shelleyolaters; I made no such rash statement or insinuation. I have been merely the humble reporter of what Miss Clairmont said to me; and if you choose to put nasty ungenerous constructions upon this, that is no fault of mine. You will remember, if you have attentively perused my first article, that my ears were soundly boxed for a moment's aberration of faith in this respect. Miss Clairmont told me that those relations were always *tout ce qu'il y a de plus platonique*; and if I did not always believe what a lady told me, that was surely a very practical incentive to faith. But one of my Shelleyolater critics really makes me smile a little at his naïvete, because he says that the insinuation (or rather more than an insinuation) made by Byron in his letter to Hoppner as to Shelley's relations with Miss Clairmont could not possibly have any truth in it, because Shelley denied it with indignation in a letter which is extant. But, my dear Shelleyolater, men who are gentlemen have a way of denying these things, it is the only kind of lie that beseems a gentleman's lips; besides Shelley's indignation, if you will kindly refer to his letter, was not caused by the suggestion that he might be on terms of greater intimacy with Miss Clairmont than desirable in a well-regulated household, but by the suggestion that she had had a child by him which had been sent to the Florence Foundling and this was quite a mistake, so far in any case, as Shelley was concerned. The rights of the story are known to myself, and I do not intend to say anything further thereon until 1901, when owing to the publication of the Hobhouse Memoirs I shall be at liberty to deal with Clairmont matters in full, eight years earlier than my promise to the lady would otherwise have permitted me. I must say this much, however, that all these Shelleyolater critics seem singularly ignorant of the feminine disposition. Women rarely make pointblank statements, especially about so delicate a thing as love; they are not logical, bless their sweet hearts! My critics would appear to wish them as prosaic as if love were to be ladled out, like tea or bacon, by the pound.

In any case, everything connected with Shelley seems to bear the same ethereal hallmark as his poetry.

It has been remarked several times to be singular that I should, at the early age of twenty, have been upon sufficiently intimate terms with Miss Clairmont to have gained her confidence to the extent I did, and that none of the residents in Florence at the time should have succeeded in doing so; but, as regards my age, that was probably a good deal in my favour, for I may say without vanity now that I was a decidedly good-looking boy in those days, with dark curly locks clustering over a marble brow, as the old novels put it, instead of as now a wisp of dingy grey fringing a wide expanse where all is brow. Old ladies often will make pets of boys when a man of forty would not be in the betting, to use a sporting phrase.

As to the residents in Florence, they were much too taken up with their lawn tennis (which had then just come in) and afternoon tea-parties and scandal to think much of the old associations of the town, or of the survivals of a great past who might still live there. And they were used to celebrities of all kinds; it was not so very long before that a genius contemporary with Byron and Shelley and Keats, whom some, ridiculously enough! put on a level with them, had passed away in Florence: Walter Savage Landor.

Miss Clairmont, in any case, persistently refused to receive almost anyone, which whetted my desire to speak face to face with this wonderful survival of the past. Such people as she did know looked upon her as a very amiable, if rather eccentric, old

b   xvii

lady, and thought little else of the matter, though the one thing which surprised all was her still marvellous beauty.

I may mention that I first learned that such a lady still lived, while reading the *World* newspaper in the English Club at Pau, and shortly afterwards travelled from thence to Florence for the express purpose of making her acquaintance. With Mr Severn, of course, my relations were quite different. I called upon him three times, that was all. He was a dear old man; but as regards him I have nothing to add to what I have already said in my article entitled "Keats and Severn." The main piece of novel information I have been able to place before the public as regards Mr Severn or Keats is that the news, through the publication of the Fanny Brawne correspondence, that the death of Keats was caused by this infatuation, was as much of a surprise (and in his case shock) to Mr Severn as to the rest of the world.

I have only to add that I have divided the book into four chapters, so as to present a more connected whole than if the actual "review" form were preserved, but the first two chapters were originally articles in the numbers of the *Nineteenth Century* for November 1893 and January 1894, with the same title as that under which they now appear. The Keats and Severn paper appeared in *The New Review* (now defunct) while under the editorship of Mr Archibald Grove, and the last and most important of the whole series, "The Secret of the Byron Separation," in the at present moribund *Twentieth Century* in 1895.

Under the promise I gave Miss Clairmont, I am precluded from writing more in connection with her confidences until 1901—that year which Matthew Arnold has prophetically said will witness a general stocktaking of the poetry of the century with a view to an award of the poetic crown. The great critic foretold Byron as the successful competitor from the shades; and perhaps he was right. To my mind (and perhaps, having known, as I did, the last two links, except Trelawney, which bound the present generation to these three wonderful poets, I have a right to speak)—to my mind, then, Keats, supreme artist as he was, is not entitled by the body of his work to rank with the other two, and my opinion as to its quality I have given in my fourth chapter. Between the other two it would be almost an impossible task to decide, so different are their claims; but I think that unless some new dazzling poetic star should spring up on the horizon between now and 1901 (and there is no time to lose), the century's poetic crown must be awarded to one or other, or that they must be dually crowned as the poetic *dioscuri* of the nineteenth century. Apart from their work the glamour of their lives is such that their names will never fade from men's memories. When other poets of the age shall have become mere names, the memory of the divine singer who found beautiful death, so longed for, among the wine-dark waves of that tideless sea whose shores were the dim empires of forgotten ages, and the soldier bard who gained the oft-desired hero's death in that Greece which had first fixed his young fancy, will be still quick and thrilling.

Until 1901, therefore, my pen must be idle on this subject, and then when all restrictions are removed, and on the dawn of a new century, I shall have my final word to say.

WILLIAM GRAHAM.

September 1898.

CHATS WITH JANE CLERMONT

IT is years ago now, and almost seems like some deep, sweet dream of bygone ages, so coloured is the reminiscence by the shades of two poets, since, when a boy in my early twenties, filled with enthusiasm for Byron and Shelley, I journeyed from the extreme south-west of France to Florence to see Jane Clermont—the once brilliant and *espiègle* Jane Clermont, who had witched the two greatest poets of our country with her loveliness and her charm. No doubt youthful ambition as well as natural curiosity impelled me, for I knew well how difficult of access the lady was. I knew that, though Trelawney, the Guiccioli, and others, who had taken part in the life-drama of the mighty poets (that short and stormy life-drama, interspersed at intervals with oases of pure delight and pleasant companionship), had proved ready enough of access, this lady alone had resolutely declined to see anyone. None of the numberless Shelleyan and Byronian biographers and critics had succeeded in obtaining a hearing from the once arch enchantress and now religious recluse from that world of which she had once been one of the gayest worldlings. And the more I thought of this, the more did I, Shelley and Byron mad, determine that, *coûte que coûte*, I would see her.

And so it befell that one spring day in 1878 I found myself, after much manœuvring and correspondence and intervention of priests, strolling on my way to the abode of Jane Clermont. It was one of those divine spring mornings, when all nature seems to burst forth into a revel of awakening life, so characteristic of the Italian spring, and so different to ours, with its softer, subtler beauties, equally lovely though they may be. The city of Lorenzo and Savonarola glowed in the golden light, and Shelley's description of Italy's awakening spring, in his letter to Leigh Hunt, was irresistibly brought back to my mind. I arrived at last at the old dark Italian house, and, on inquiring for the lady who was the object of my visit, was shown into an old-fashioned sixteenth-century room, which served as sitting-room, and informed that the signora would be with me presently. Meantime, I passed my time in looking round the room: it was a quaint, dark, old Italian room, furnished in ultra-Italian style, but not in the style of the Italy of to-day, rather that of the thirties or forties; and on the walls were two Madonnas and several crucifixes, beside one of which, by a strange irony, hung a portrait of Shelley—Shelley, the arch poetical iconoclast! What would he have said to "Claire" amid such surroundings? At last a lady entered, and a strange thrill passed over me as the vision of so many of my boyish dreams stood before me in flesh and blood, and Byron and Shelley became as men I had known myself.

"Good-morning," she said, with a sprightly smile, all out of keeping with those eighty years of life. "So, you seem determined to see me?"

"Madame, I have travelled here from the other side of France to do so," I replied. "It would indeed have been hard had you persisted in your denial."

"Ah, curiosity, curiosity!" the lady replied. "I think our mother Eve bequeathed that quality in quite as bountiful measure to her sons as to her daughters. Well, my young friend, I condole with you, coming here, no doubt, with dreams of Shelley and Mary and their poor Claire (who was, I may say without vanity now, a beautiful woman once) and finding a wretched, worn-out old creature on the threshold of the unknown.

> Oh life, oh time!
> On whose last steps I climb,

as our dear Percy said."

I protested indignantly.

"Madame! you are beautiful now as ever; and there is no age for those who have known Shelley, and whom he loved. I am young now, but never, if I live to a century, shall I have a greater privilege

3

than this, to see the Constantia of Shelley, whose voice was as sweet as the poet's song."

She smiled sweetly at my white heat of boyish fervour, and told me to be seated.

What I had said as to beauty was true enough. She was a lovely old lady: the eyes were still bright, and sparkled at times with irony and fun; the complexion clear as at eighteen, and the lovely white hair as beautiful in its way as the glossy black tresses of youth must have been; the slender willowy figure had remained unaltered, as though time itself had held that sacred and passed by—a true woman of the poets. Well, now, could I imagine the glorious beauty of fifty and sixty years back, and well could I appreciate the jealous rancour and malice of La Guiccioli.

"And so you persuaded the good father to intercede with me," she said. "Oh, what a Machiavel! It seems you actually had the audacity to tell him you were trembling on the verge of the faith, and thought an interview with me would turn the scale."

And she laughed with a very silvery laugh.

I was a little surprised, for I had been given to understand that Jane Clermont was a very fervid *religieuse*, and replied with a smile, looking round the room, "I thought the counsel of such an exemplary *dévote* would solve all my doubts and lull all my troubles with the 'eternal croon' of Rome."

4

The lady was down upon me with that sharpness which amused the Shelleys, but which the spoiled Byron detested, and, no doubt, led to the eventual separation.

"When you make quotations, my young friend," she said, "you should always take care to mention the original source ; however, 'eternal croon' exactly represents the influence of Rome on storm-beaten, chequered lives like mine. There comes a time when one is glad not to have the trouble of reasoning—indeed, to have it forbidden—and to resign oneself to blind faith as to sleep."

I smiled, and replied, " I can believe this, madame, of some people, but surely not of the critical, witty Jane Clermont, who seems much the same now as in the days of Shelley."

"Oh no! My poor old mind has undergone many a shock since those days," said she. "I feel that I must have something to lean upon. Roman Catholicism is such a comforting religion, and I receive so much comfort from that dear father."

It seemed to me that the lady's religion was not very deeply ingrained, and it struck me as particularly strange ; one of her greatest complaints against Byron in the past having been that he brought her daughter up in the very religion of which she was now, in exterior at least, such an enthusiastic practitioner. Of course, however, I could not allude to this extremely delicate subject, and I contented myself with remarking:

5

"What would Shelley say could he revisit the glimpses of the moon, and see his beloved Claire an abhorred Christian?"

"I don't know," she replied. "I think Shelley would have forgiven me anything; and I am not sure that the thought of him did not lead to the thought of Christ. How strange it all seems now, when at last he is appreciated as perhaps the greatest poet of all time, to think how I used to box his ears and tease his life out!"

A glint of sunshine passed, and the sweet Italian breeze blew in at the open window.

"What a heavenly day!" she exclaimed. "How these perfect Italian days remind me of him, and of Mary! It seems almost impossible that such an abyss of years can have passed since that awful day when I first heard the news from Spezzia. And this is the same Italy, the same Italy," she continued, dreamily; "and yet how different from the Italy that he knew! but the same Italy; and I live here still because it is sanctified to me by his memory."

"As you are to me," I replied. "I feel, I think, the same sweet strangeness in looking upon you that you must in looking upon Florence, and then back through the years. Do you remember those lines of Browning——"

But she interrupted with:

> "Did you see Shelley face to face,
> And did he stop and speak to you?
> How strange it seems, and new!

6

Is that what you mean?" she said.

"Yes, madame," I replied. "I feel in talking with you as though I were speaking with someone who had been loved by the gods. I cannot explain to you the strange, weird feeling that I experience."

"How he would have loved a morning like this!" she exclaimed, turning from the open window, with a bright smile and a soft sigh. "I can see him now running in like a boy 'drenched with the joy of spring-time,' to use his own expression. He loved spring best of all the seasons." And then, looking at me with a smile, she said:

"Ah! primavera gioventu del anno;
Ah! gioventu primavera del vita.

That man was not like any other. There did not seem to be any separation in him from nature; he was as a part of it."

And then we fell-to talking about Shelley; and so fascinating was the subject that, though I had paid my visit by appointment at eleven, it was nearly one by the time I had an opportunity of departing on my way; and then the lady insisted that I should remain to her *déjeûner*, which she took at one. A charming little lunch we had, by an open window embosomed in flowers.

Although Miss Clermont had, as I knew, lost most of the money which Shelley had left her in the Lumley Italian Opera House disaster, yet she had evidently still sufficient to keep her in perfect comfort, and even luxury. The *déjeûner* was served in a fashion which showed plainly that my hostess was accustomed to the good things of life ; and the Chianti was a dream.

At last, I rose to wish my kind hostess adieu. I had not heard half what I had wanted to hear, but my position was a very delicate one. With a man it would have been different : there are so many things that one can ask of one's own sex that it would be impossible to ask or even mention to a lady. I had never alluded to the name of Byron, and our talk of Shelley had been merely in the general way above described. I was intensely grateful and flattered by the charming courtesy with which I had been received ; but disappointed, for I had hoped to have heard more.

However, I had seen and conversed with the beloved of the gods, and that was something that no one else had done.

"Good-bye, madame," I said. "I cannot thank you sufficiently for your kindness, and the honour you have paid me. Believe me, I shall never forget either."

But, to my surprise and delight, she said, "*Au revoir*, but not adieu. You have come all the way from England to see me, and do you think I am going to let you run away like this ? "

"I would not be the first, madame," I meekly replied.

8

"Perhaps not," she said; "but I feel I can depend upon you. I have been keeping great watch on you all the time"—and again that merry, silvery laugh on which old age seemed to have no power —"and I know that there are dozens of questions I could see you were dying to ask, but tact prevailed. No, I would never see anyone; for" (and a blush coloured the still beautiful tracery of the skin) "I do not wish to be made, *nolens volens*, the subject of a Byron-Shelley controversy. If, however, you will treat me as a friend, and promise me that you will, if you feel inclined to write, publish nothing of me until ten years after my death, and certain things that I will tell you not till thirty years afterwards, I will make a clean breast of everything to you. Will that suit you, signor?" she asked, with another bewitching smile.

"I can only say, madame," I replied, "that you will confer on me the greatest pleasure that I have ever received, or ever will receive. I give my promise, and you may depend upon the promise being absolutely kept."

"I know that," the lady replied, "or I would not have made the offer I did. Then I shall expect you here every day while you are in Florence. I go out very little, but usually either between eleven and one in these lovely spring mornings, or about five, to have the benefit of the Italian evenings, which are equally sweet."

It was agreed that I should call for her the next

9

afternoon at five, and that we should go for a drive in the Lung Arno.

On returning to my hotel I made a note of the various matters about which I wished to converse with her. First: I wished to know the circumstances relating to her original meeting with Byron, and the growth of the intimacy. Second: As to whether there had been any acquaintance between Byron and Shelley prior to their meeting at Geneva, and whether that meeting had been in any way pre-arranged, both of which have always been moot points. Third: I wished to ascertain her feelings as to Byron and Shelley respectively, and particularly the latter, as to which there had always been so much gossip, beginning with Byron and Hoppner, and colour to which had undoubtedly been lent by Shelley's legacy of £12,000. Fourth: I wished to ascertain the general character and personal manner of the two men from the lips of one who had possessed, perhaps better than anyone, opportunities of judging them—opportunities which her quick satirical power of observation had undoubtedly not allowed her to throw away. I looked forward to these further opportunities of conversation with the liveliest pleasure; for, apart from the absolutely novel information as to these fascinating personalities and their *entourage*, I saw clearly that I should obtain, and the weird delight of conversation with this survival from the past—that strange, enchanting past of

Leman and of Italy—a past of over sixty years back, but more real than was to-day, so clothed and transfigured was it by the dazzling light of poetry; besides all this, there was in the lady herself a charm which old age could not kill— a charm that must once have been all-powerful. I looked forward to next day's drive almost as much for that reason as for what I should hear.

There were no signs of old age about this woman of the poets, except the white hair; the voice was as clear as a bell, the hearing and intellect as acute as ever, and the eyes as bright. It was a rare privilege.

The next day, at five, I called in the carriage for Miss Clermont, and we drove together along the Lung Arno.

"It must seem strange and dream-like to you," I said, "driving along this road, which you must have known so well with Shelley and Mary, with a wretched latter nineteenth-century man."

"No doubt the downcome is great," she replied, with that wicked smile which youth had passed on to age undiminished in malice and in mirth; "but yes, as you say, it seems all like a dream: perhaps after all, as Shelley said, life is only a dream. I seriously rather tend to believe that. The past seems so much more real than the present. Do you know those words of Goëthe's?—

> Was neu geschah das seh' ich wie im weiten,
> Und was verschwand wird mir zur Wirklichkeiten.

11

They are the only words I know which exactly express what I mean ; but you will feel just the same when you are my age."

"Ah, madame! I trust that will not be," I said. "Over you the years pass by, as by one sacred to the gods, as though time himself had enjoined them to pass only in play ; and when death comes at last, he will come, oh, so softly! But the years do not deal thus with others, and I should have no glorious memories—memories annihilating time —to look back upon."

"Ah, but I long for death!" she said. "Death represents to me all that is beautiful and to be desired. The mere objective view of it is pleasing to me — blissful, changeless rest. Ah! my child, may you never grow to want rest, rest, rest, as I do! But I do believe what we call death has vastly deeper meanings than mere repose," she continued. "I believe, with Shelley, that it is but the gateway to worlds and worlds of infinite possibilities, and not for one single moment do I ever doubt that I shall meet my beloved one again. To speak of annihilation in connection with Shelley seems mere rank absurdity. I do not believe anyone who once knew that man could do so."

"Then, holding these ideas, what need for the 'eternal croon'?" I said.

The lady replied Socratic-like by another question : "Why take opium or haschish?"

"Tell me now of Shelley and Byron," I requested.

At the last name, the first time I had mentioned it, a momentary frown contracted her brow.

"Of course," she said, "you know how unpleasant any mention of that man is to me, and I appreciate your delicacy in making no allusion to him until I had promised to tell you everything."

"But surely he was a great man, and a noble character, despite his faults," I said; "and you are too large-minded to bear hate beyond the grave."

"I bear no hate," was her reply, "only absolute indifference, and a great deal of contempt in some respects; and the subject is naturally unpleasant. I see you quite misunderstand matters, as probably most people do. Hate follows often very close on the heels of love; but I never loved Byron."

And before I could reply she stopped my mouth with those "snowy fingers" of Constantia, which were youthful yet, saying:

"Listen! and I will tell you the whole story. It is perhaps as well that it should be told at last, and then you can, if you please, make the right facts known after the time I have told you to wait has elapsed. The real facts never have been known yet, and none of the biographers have been right."

This is the story she told me.

"In 1815, when I was a very young girl, Byron was the rage. When I say the rage, I mean what you people nowadays can perhaps hardly conceive. I suppose no man who ever lived has possessed the extraordinary celebrity of Lord Byron in such an intense, haunting, almost maddening degree. And this celebrity extended all over the Continent to as great an extent as in England; and, remember, in those days there were no railways or telegraphs."

I interpolated here: "Even now, when there are railways and telegraph-wires everywhere, none of our writers are much known abroad. It is very curious, sometimes, when mentioning some well-known English writer's name to a foreigner, to find he has never heard it, although one had thought the renown European. I suppose Tennyson is the only present English writer whose fame is European."

"Yes," replied she; "but Tennyson has never had the same kind of fame as Byron. His has been a steady, equable light; Byron's was a short, fierce, blinding glare: and, as I say, all Europe was so enthralled with the magic of the man's very name, that the sensation he made even discounted, to some extent, the sensation of Waterloo. It was a troubling, morbid obsession, the influence he exercised over all, and especially over the youth of England of both sexes. The young poetasters used to imitate his dress and appearance as far as they could, and the girls made simple idiots of themselves about him. Numberless letters used to come to him daily, often of the most absurd description, from the languishing fair. He usually converted them into cigar-lights: at that time he had rather a fancy for cigar-smoking, which he gave up later on.

"Well, at the time when he was at the very height of his fame, and I was a young girl, filled with all kinds of fancies, encouraged instead of checked by the circle in which I lived—Godwin and my sister (as I always was taught to call her), Mary Shelley, and Shelley himself, who floated in and out of the house with his wild notions and sweet ways, like some unearthly spirit; in the days when Byron was manager of Drury Lane Theatre, I bethought myself that I would go on to the stage. Our means were very narrow, and it was necessary for me to do something, and this seemed to suit me better than anything else ; in any case, it was the only form of occupation congenial to my girlish love of glitter and excitement. I think it was Shelley who first of all suggested my applying to Byron, and it is very probable that the suggestion came in that way, for Shelley was Byron-mad at that time, and Byron's verses were always on his lips; indeed, Shelley up to the last was a most ⸱ enthusiastic admirer of Byron, although I believe it is the fashion among certain critics nowadays to say the reverse. His admiration of *the man* wore off, no doubt, and for the same reasons that mine did, and the fact of knowing *the man* as well as he did no doubt coloured his admiration of *the poet*, which was once idolatry; but his admiration 'on this side idolatry,' as Ben Johnson said of Shakespeare, remained unchanged. I called, then, on Byron in his capacity of manager, and he promised to do what he could to help me as regards the stage.

The result you know. I am too old now to play
with any mock repentance. I was young, and vain,
and poor. He was famous beyond all precedent, so
famous that people, and especially young people,
hardly considered him as a man at all, but rather
as a god. His beauty was as haunting as his fame,
and he was all-powerful in the direction in which
my ambition turned. It seems to me almost need-
less to say that the attentions of a man like this,
with all London at his feet, very quickly completely
turned the head of a girl in my position ; and when
you recollect that I was brought up to consider
marriage not only as a useless but as an absolutely
sinful custom, that only bigotry made necessary,
you will scarcely wonder at the result, which you
know. Whatever may have been my faults, I have
never been given to cant, and I do not intend to
begin now at eighty. A few months after my
first meeting with Byron the final crash came, and
he left England. The time during which I knew
him in England was the time of the avalanche of
his misfortunes, when he had disappeared from the
world, when London was raging against him, and
he saw almost no one but me.

"Shortly before Byron left England, in April
1816, I went with Shelley and Mary to Geneva.
No doubt you have read about our previous peculiar
expedition, the year before, the Waterloo year,"
she added, with a laugh. " How we traversed France
in a donkey-chaise. Oh dear, dear ! What a happy,

funny time it was, and what queer places we stopped at sometimes!"

"Yes; you must have had great fun," I replied. "I have often thought how glorious it would have been to have been one of the party. Tell me now, please, a thing which no one seems to have settled. There is a house in Marlow which has the inscription on the outside to the effect that Shelley lived there, and was visited there by Lord Byron, above a quotation from Shelley's *Adonais*. Is this the case? Did Shelley know Byron before they met in Geneva, and did Byron ever visit him there? All the biographers seem to insist that they never saw one another before the meeting in Geneva, and that Shelley only took the house after returning from Geneva, whereas Byron never returned to England again."

"Quite right," she replied. "But we spent a great deal of the summer and autumn of 1815 on the river, although it was not their head-quarters; in fact, it was on account of the fancy that Shelley took to Marlow, and to the house, in the Waterloo year, that we settled there at the very end of the year following.

"Dear old place, how well I remember it, and the sweet garden, too! Tell me, is that there still?"

"Yes, yes," I replied. "Many a time I have made pilgrimages to Marlow for the purpose of lying on the mound at the end of the garden through a summer afternoon, because they told me that Shelley wrote and read there. Is that true?"

"Quite true," she replied. "He would spend hours on that mound. How well I can picture his graceful, boyish figure reclining there with his favourite Plato, or Sophocles, or Spenser, with the beautiful English sunlight playing on him! Oh, what lovely days we had on that dear river! Mary and Shelley, of course, lived by it, and I used to run down every now and then, and lived with them on returning from Geneva. Ah, how well I can remember that coach and that sweet, breezy English country between London and Marlow! I have seen much beautiful scenery since, but never anything to surpass Marlow and Medmenham, and The Bisham and Quarry woods. We lived entirely in the open air, picnicking in our boats and in the woods. Shelley wrote *Alastor*, I remember, at that time, and a great part of *The Revolt of Islam*, and almost entirely in the open air. Do people go much along the river now?"

"Oh yes, madame, they do indeed!" I said: "but it is a very different matter now. Marlow is only an hour from London by rail, and the river from Kingston to Oxford swarms with cheap trippers, while stucco villas are springing up every-where; but it is very lovely still, and some parts are quite unspoiled, Marlow being one of them, I am happy to say."

"Is the old inn there still—The Crown?"

"Most certainly," I replied. "When, in fits of Shelley-mania, I make my pilgrimages to Marlow, I always stop there. Is it not a sweet, quaint, old place? I do not know how it appeared in the days when you were at Marlow; but to me, a being of this bustling, feverish railroad age, it seems the quintessence of rest and peace. Many is the drowsy day — those river days which, as Tennyson says, 'are always afternoon' — that I have dreamed away there."

"And have you reserved all your enthusiasm for Shelley, for the old house and the mound, and reserved none for the inn?"

"Well, I must say," I answered, "I never thought much of Shelley in connection with it. To begin with, I knew he was a water-drinker, and he seems far too ethereal a creature to connect with the good English ale which has always been the pride of The Crown. There are other great geniuses whom one readily connects with old English inns, but Shelley is hardly one of them."

Jane Clermont laughed merrily.

"But we girls 'had no objection' to an occasional 'pot of ale,' as your dear friend Byron put it (for I can see you are an idolater at that shrine); we often had our meals in the inn, and were constantly in and out. I remember there was a big dog always about in the garden we made a great pet of. I can see Shelley now coming from the river into that little inn-parlour, and his comical face of disgust when he found us taking anything of an alcoholic nature and meat food, and the landlord's good-humoured banter of the poet, who would live on lettuces and lemonade. Why, it was really at that inn that the first meeting between Byron and Shelley took place, in August 1815."

"Indeed!" I exclaimed, with astonishment; "that will certainly endow it with a new interest for everyone. Tell me how was that?"

"In this way," she continued. "I had told him much of Shelley, and he delightedly fell in with my proposal to accompany me one day when I had arranged to visit the Shelleys at Marlow, where they were then stopping, a few days. We started early one morning—a most unusual thing for Byron to do, for he went to bed about the time when Shelley left his, but this time he made an exception—and we arrived at Marlow about the mid-day dinner-hour. They told us at the house that Shelley and Mary were on the river, but had left word that they would be in the inn at two o'clock, when they expected to meet me. Byron refreshed himself meantime with a huge mug of beer—I remember well thinking how horrified the worshippers of the ethereal poet would have been— and hobbled after me through Marlow, which he had not seen before. We very soon returned to the inn, as his lame leg made walking almost an impossibility.

A few minutes afterwards in came Shelley and Mary. It was such a merry party that we made at lunch in the inn parlour : Byron was in the spirits of a boy, and Shelley was overjoyed at meeting his idolised poet, who had actually come all the way from London to see him. The conversation varied from maddest fun and frolic to grave subjects of 'fate, free-will, and destiny,' and Shelley was great on the contrast between the beauty of the scenery about us and what he considered the degraded condition of the English peasantry. 'Imagine scenes like these!' I remember him saying, 'peopled by beings fit to inhabit them, as, by the uprooting of a few tyrannous customs and debasing superstitions, another generation might make them.' 'Pooh!' replied Byron, 'your poetry, my dear Mr Shelley, is lovely ; but your ideas are, if you will pardon me, Utopian. You may do with mankind what you please, but you will never make it anything else than the unsavoury congeries of dupes and thieves that it is and always will be. You might as well talk of implanting philanthropic sentiments in the mind of a monkey, or tender sentiments in that of a tiger, as of developing man into an angel, which is practically what you suggest. Indeed, man is a great deal worse than either. He is the only brute which kills from aimless brutish-ness.' I have never forgotten those words," she added ; "they give the keynotes to the two men's characters."

The lady then repeated to me fragments from

many conversations between Byron and Shelley, without any of the pretensions made by some contemporaries of both to absolute accuracy, but with probably far more claim to it than most, for she had a marvellous memory. I am afraid I was constantly teasing her for conversations at different times between the two great poets, and she always replied, with a smile :

"You must remember I did not note down all they said at the time, as you say you do with my immortal words, but this is what was said, as far as I can remember, and I think I am not far wrong."

Perhaps at some future time I may be inclined to give some of these dialogues to the world ; for if she did not note them down at the time, I certainly did do so, as they came from her lips, on returning each evening to my own abode, with the words fresh in my memory, and showed her the following day what I had written.

Byron, she said, on the occasion of his visit to Marlow remained the night at the inn, and left next day for London by the coach. Early the following year all was arranged for the meeting in Geneva. At last, therefore, this matter is set at rest, as it could have been by me any time since Jane Clermont's death, had I not given the beforementioned promise to her.

"Did Shelley and Mary altogether approve, then, of this intimacy ?" I asked.

"Most certainly," she replied, briefly. "I have already told you—what you know, of course, already—what the Shelleys' opinions on these matters were, or what Shelley's were, because Mary docilely followed his lead in these things; and in a lasting union, as he hoped it would be, between his sister-in-law, as he always called me, and a man whom he at that time considered almost as a god, he saw nothing but what should ardently be desired. He thought that I would be to Byron what Mary was to him. Alas, alas! little did any one of us understand what Byron really was then."

"But Shelley married Mary as soon as he could?"

"Yes," she replied; "to gratify Godwin's wish. Of course, as you know, Godwin, as described in *The Revolt of Islam*, was his idol; but he none the less, and always, distinctly disapproved of marriage as an institution."

And now our drive was over. We passed through the city of flowers, dome and cupola gilded by the soft light of the setting sun; and further conversation was postponed until next day.

Next day it was arranged that I was to call again for Miss Clermont for a drive, explore Florence by myself in the afternoon, and dine with her in the evening at seven. So at eleven o'clock I called, and we had a lovely drive, sauntering later through the Medici galleries, and I parted with her at her door, at which I again presented myself at seven. I found this time that I was not the only guest, for a charming and beautiful young lady, a great favourite of Miss Clermont's, was also present— an English girl of Scottish parentage. The Byron-Shelley subject was dropped for the nonce, and we talked of Italy and the Italians.

"I have lived so long in Italy," said Jane Clermont, "ever since I lost my money in that idiotic Opera House affair in London, before either of you were born, that I almost feel an Italian myself."

"You certainly look one," I replied; "that struck me at the very first. You must surely have some Italian blood in your veins."

"Not that I am aware of," she said; "but one never knows. Unless one belongs to some historic family it is difficult to say what blood one has or what one has not."

Notwithstanding her recluse life, Madame Clermont evidently kept herself well *au courant* with what was going on, and we spent a most enjoyable evening, talking about all sorts and conditions of things. Mr Gladstone was evidently her great latter-day hero as a man of action, and again and again she recurred to the subject of Tennyson as a poet. She was also well acquainted with Mr Swinburne's works, and on my remarking that he was the most musical of all our poets, surpassing in absolute musical cadence, as distinct from rhythm pure and simple, Shelley or Tennyson themselves, she asked me to recite the verse of his I considered most musical. I remember I repeated this:

> "If you were I and I were you—
> How should I love you—say?
> How should the rose-leaf love the rue?
> The day love nightfall and her dew?
> Though night may love the day."

"That, I think, madame," I said, "is for absolute melody—melody ringing clear as a bell—unequalled in the language, unless it be by one or two of Keats's odes."

"Then you do not consider even Shelley equal to Swinburne as a melodist?" she asked me.

"No; I do not," I replied. "As an absolute melodist—I mean a master of word-music as distinct from other qualities — I consider Swinburne unequalled. As a poet I hold Shelley infinitely superior to anyone living. I personally consider him, as a *poet*, the king of all. No poet of any time or land is worthy to sit upon that throne. A pity he wasted so much of his short life over matters that did not relate to his art at all."

"Ah, but you are wrong there!" she replied. "Had it not been for his intense love of mankind, that fervid zeal of his which could not content itself with poetry alone, he would never have been the great poet you admire."

25

"Perhaps not," I replied; "but surely there is a good deal in his works, especially in *The Revolt of Islam*, more suited to the lecture-room than to the poem. How different when he steps into that dazzling realm of pure poetry! How different is *Epipsychidion*, or *The Ode to the West Wind*, or to *The Skylark!*"

And she broke in with a voice that was as silvery as Mr Gladstone's * is now:

"With thy clear calm joyance
        Languor cannot be :
    Shadow of annoyance
        Never came near thee :
Thou lovest, but ne'er knew love's sad satiety."

"Ah, madame!" I said, "but the most beautiful of any is to Constantia singing. If I could only have heard Constantia singing, I should have asked for nothing else from life."

"Ah!" she said, with a little half-regretful, half-amused laugh, "poor Constantia can sing no more now, and she is following her voice to the mysterious beyond. But here is someone who will supply the place of Constantia."

And then a strange thing happened.

The young lady took her place at the piano, and began to sing a touching Scottish song—I forget

* The articles forming this book were begun in 1893 and ended in 1895.

the name, but I remember the last verses so well by what took place:

"Could ye come back to me, Douglas, Douglas!
    In the old likeness that I knew,
I would be so tender, so loving, Douglas,
    Douglas, Douglas! tender and true.

Never a scornful word should pain you,
    I'd smile as sweet as angels do,
Sweet as your smile on me shone ever,
    Douglas, Douglas! tender and true.

Stretch out your hand to me, Douglas, Douglas!
    Rain forgiveness from Heaven like dew,
As I lay my heart on thy dead heart, Douglas,
    Douglas, Douglas! tender and true."

When these verses were sung with that clear, sweet voice, we both noticed that our dear hostess had completely broken down. She was crying bitterly, as if her heart would break, but oh so gracefully!—not like an old lady might cry, but like some young girl with her first love sorrow.

"Don't mind me, dears," she said. "I'm in one of my silly moods to-night. I'm only a miserable old woman who feels very lonely at times. I think you know what memories that song brought back," she added, looking at me; and then turning to her young friend, "Sing something else, darling. Her voice is so sweet, is it not, Mr Graham?"

"I almost feel that I am listening to Constantia singing," I replied.

And then this young lady, who would have nought to do with aught but pathetic ballads, began on

27

that divine song of Villon's, *Où sont les neiges d'antan?* set to a soft, sweet melody, and the voice rose and fell with a dreamy cadence.

"Ah! where are they indeed," said our hostess, "the great men I have known, and the burning words I have heard, and the stormy times? *Où sont les neiges d'antan?*" she repeated, musingly. "What a dream life is, to be sure!"

During my stay in Florence we met constantly, for I was given *mes entrées* without restriction, and where I had expected to meet an old and morose *dévote*, I found a lady so witty and so *piquante* that one absolutely forgot her age. But I did not wonder at her earning the reputation she had, for she was absolutely world-weary, and, with the exception of a pet priest or two (whom she laughed at, moreover), she would see no one; and, as I have already said, her powers of satire, and even mimicry, remained unimpaired. I could well understand the shortness of her connection with the sensitive, spoiled Byron, who had been accustomed to pose as a God to the womankind of London. Her powers of mimicry amused me immensely. I had not, and have not, the most graceful gait in the world; indeed, my so-called walk partakes more of the nature of a shuffle, arising from a peculiar, not precisely malformation, but weakness in the knees, and this she hit off in the most amusing manner. I should, perhaps, apologise for introducing this piece of personality, but that it suddenly flashed across me at the time that perchance I had hit upon the whole secret of Byron's intense aversion to her, following on a romantic passion. Byron's sensitiveness as to his lameness is, of course, notorious, and it is well known how the devoted Fletcher said to Trelawney, at the end of all at Missolonghi, pointing to the corpse's limbs: "All my lord's misfortunes are due to that."

I asked her plainly, " Did you ever mimic Byron's lameness, madame?" and she replied, "No, I don't think so," but added, " I may have done so, though, sometimes to others. We were all often hurried about our expeditions, and he generally hobbled up late."

That remark, I thought, might mean a good deal.

Sitting one day by the Arno, I asked her the reason of her prejudice against Byron and her strong affection for Shelley.

" As I have already said," she replied, " I have no prejudice against Byron. He behaved atrociously to me ; but that was my own fault—I ought to have known better — or perhaps misfortune would be the better word, for I was too young to have any knowledge of character. All those reports about rancour were set about by La Guiccioli. Naturally a woman does not like to have her child taken from her, and to be left almost without means. I suppose you are as crass as most men, and think that I loved Byron ?"

I made no reply.

"My young friend, no doubt you will know a woman's heart better some day. I was dazzled; but that does not mean love. It might, perhaps, have grown into love; but it never did."

"Have you never loved, madame?" I asked.

A delicate blush suffused the cheeks, and this time she made no reply, gazing on the ground.

"Shelley?" I murmured.

"With all my heart and soul," she replied, without moving her eyes from the ground.

"Perhaps," I said later, "Byron's bad conduct had something to do with this; he seems to have been very acute."

"I have said that he told lies about Shelley," she replied, "things without a word of truth," she added with feminine tautology. "Why do you smile?"

"At my thoughts, madame," I said.

"And what may they be?"

"Ah! you cannot force me to tell them, imperious as you are. Surely one's thoughts are free?"

"I do command you!" she insisted.

"Well then, madame, if you command, I must of course, obey. I was thinking of a line of Shakespeare's."

"And the line?"

"'Methinks the lady doth protest too much.'"

"You impertinent boy! If you do not believe what I tell you, why traverse Europe to see me?"

"There are things, madame," I said, "which it is the duty of every man to believe when told him by a lady, and I have conquered my scepticism. I remember you told me Shelley was a devoted student of Plato."

Two smart boxes on the ear were the only reply I received to this. A sorry return, indeed, for obedience and faith.

It was impossible to obtain a good word for Byron from this lady, though, to do her justice, she showed no rancour, and I must admit I gradually began to feel my hero's stature dwarfing; but I was young then and impressionable, and, since, I have restored him to his old position in my affections.

"He was utterly selfish," she said; but she could not deny that he gave about a third of his money away to the poor.

"Well, he did not show much generosity to that unfortunate Leigh Hunt," she insisted; and on my replying that, after all, Leigh Hunt must have been rather a vulgar cockney bore, she riposted with, "It is, after all, natural that you should take up the cudgels for Byron, for he was a thorough Scot; his brilliancy and good looks he inherited, to a great extent, from the 'gay Gordons,' his mother's family, and his love of the bawbees and his love of dogmatic religion were both intensely Scottish. He had 'scotched, not killed the Scotsman in his blood,' as he himself said in *Don Juan*, with a vengeance.

31

He even wanted to secure both this world and the next in some canny Scotch fashion. He would talk religion and predestination and other exploded doctrines with any old Presbyterian parson by the hour, without the remotest idea of practising any religion whatsoever; though, to do him justice, he was not in the least afraid of death. In fact, he was absolutely reckless of life."

"Well, you must admit that the final scene, the fight for Greece, was splendid?"

" I don't know that there was anything particularly splendid about it," she replied. "He was tired to death of La Guiccioli, whom he treated in a way very few women would have stood, notwithstanding the rapturous memoirs she wrote of him some years ago; and he simply invested a great deal of money in the Greek cause with the idea of being made a king, which, as Trelawney says, he undoubtedly would have been if he had lived, notwithstanding his stern republicanism.

"Byron was a great poetic genius and an extremely able man, and, in his way, a thorough man of the world, but he was utterly selfish, utterly false, and utterly spoiled and vain, while, as the French say, he was always playing to the gallery. That is my opinion, anyhow, and you may take it for what it is worth."

I took it for what it was worth. Byron had treated her badly, as Shelley had treated Harriett Westbrook. Under the circumstances, I think she was more just than the majority of women would have been.

In reply to questions from me as to the exterior manner and appearance of the two men, she said that Byron was a great deal of a dandy, though latterly more of a foreign than an English dandy, his stay abroad having much more denationalised him than Shelley's had him. Byron had become very Italian in his habits. The manners of both were perfect— the easy, unassuming manner of well-born and brought-up English gentlemen — though Shelley's was simpler.

I asked her how they would compare with the same class nowadays. "Well," she replied, "you see I know so few of my countrymen now, but I should say just the same." There was, however, she said, a great difference between the manner of the two men, for though neither put on what is nowadays vulgarly but expressively called "side," Shelley was perfectly simple and natural, while Byron's manner, though it could be charming to a degree, was tinged with a vein of Don Juanesque reckless-ness. In fact, she said, "the stanzas of that poem convey a very good idea of Byron's manner."

Byron's great charm, she said, was his voice, which was as melodious in its subtle variety of cadence as music itself.

My interest in this lady, on account of her relations with the two great poets, grew into a very warm attachment for herself, and the parting was very painful to me. It is painful even now to look back upon that fair spring morning, when life was spring-time too, and the kind words as I almost broke down: "Oh! what a silly boy. You can come and see me again next spring, and anyhow life is only a dream. You will meet me in the after-world with Shelley—and I hope not with Byron," she added, with her humorous smile. "Come, kiss me, and say good-bye like a man. No; not good-bye, *au revoir*. *Au revoir*, dear, in this world or the next. I am sure it is only *au revoir*. Meantime, you must forget all about me."

"I shall never forget, madame," I replied, with a choking in the throat as I kissed those lips which had been kissed by Byron and by Shelley. And I never shall. But that spring-time never came, and I am waiting for the after-world; for soon after that dear lady passed

"To where beyond these voices there is peace."

CHAPTER II

THE subject-matter dealt with in these conversations must, of course, be limited by the promise of which I made mention in my previous article —to publish only information relating to certain things which were specified at the time. Many years have yet to pass ere I may be enabled to write in full of the life of Miss Clermont. Ten years from her decease, whenever that might take place, was, as I have already said, stipulated upon before she would allow me to publish anything relating to her, and even that was made dependent on the death, meantime, of Sir Percy Shelley, a death which has only comparatively recently occurred; thirty years being the time I promised to wait before publishing clearly specified matter, intensely interesting, but of a nature which I must not even hint at here.

Before proceeding further, I have some words to say relating to questions raised by reviewers of my first article, questions which the courtesy and appreciation with which I have been treated impose upon me the obligation of answering.

35

First, the question of my orthography as regards the lady's name. This has already been answered by me in the *Times*, and the proof of the accuracy of my spelling of the name *Clermont* can be seen by a glance at the British Museum catalogue.*

I must here, however, admit two little slips of my own. One is the passage in the letter referred to, where I speak of the profusion of Christian names which the lady was wont to delight in, being shown in the letter to Byron. There I am wrong. The proof of her proneness to romantic nomenclature is to be found in another and later document than the letter to Byron. In the later document she signs herself Clara Mary Constantia Jane Clairmont, the Constantia being, of course, a remembrance of the celebrated poem *To Constantia Singing*. In the letter to Byron she signs herself simply Claire, the first syllable of her surname spelt as some of my critics would have it, and both of these facts decidedly tend to bear out my suggestion that she preferred the perhaps more romantic Clairmont to Clermont. But we find the name spelt variously, as Clairmont, Clermont, Charlemont, Clairemont, and Claremont. At the time I knew her she used to prefer to be styled Clara rather than Claire. Clearly a most wayward and romantic young lady, and she preserved many

* Subsequently to the information gained for me by Sir D. E. Colnaghi, referred to in the third Chapter, I altered the spelling of the word, and it will be found spelt Clairmont in Chapters III. and IV.

of her youthful characteristics to the last, which to a great extent constituted her charm. One can well understand her dislike in youth to the homely nomenclature of Mary Jane, and it is under these names she figures in Shelley's will. She herself evidently preferred them when "washed down" by a profusion of more romantic designations.

And now let me set at rest a matter as to which there has been a good deal of dispute — namely, Miss Clermont's age when she first met Byron. Miss Clermont was born in 1798; consequently, when she met Byron in 1815, she was seventeen. I am quite aware that in saying she met Byron in 1815 I am exposing myself to the assaults of various Byronian writers who maintain that the Clermont connection did not take place until after the cessation of intercourse with Lady Byron; but they are wrong. By the way, I think it is as well to point out here a slight error made by Mr Garnett, the able and courteous keeper of printed documents in the British Museum, in his short notice of Miss Clermont. As one of my reviewers has well said, nearly everyone who has written on this subject has fallen into some error of chronology. Mr Garnett is perfectly correct as to the date of the lady's birth, but he speaks of her later on as nearly two-and-twenty in 1816. I asked Mr Garnett personally for an explanation of this, and he told me he had, in the first instance, the idea that she was born in the same year as Edward Williams, who met his death with Shelley. But even then Mr Garnett would have been wrong as to Miss Clermont's age in 1816, for Edward Williams was born in 1792—the year, by a strange coincidence, of both Shelley's and Trelawney's births. Trelawney himself relates this in his "Reminiscences of Byron and Shelley," in the course of a conversation taking place between Shelley, Williams, and himself. Miss Clermont, therefore, had Mr Garnett been correct in his first belief as to the date of her birth, would have been twenty-four, and not twenty-two, in 1816, when, according to Mr Garnett and others, she first met Byron—a view which I have already said I hold (in fact, I have shown) to be erroneous, and Miss Clermont was really the cause of Byron's divorce ; but that leads to matters upon which I must not at present deal. Mr Jeaffreson is the only writer of Byronia who suspects what I have said to have been the case, and Mr Garnett, in his notice just alluded to, calls the idea an absurd one. I do not in the least apprehend why the idea should be "absurd"; in any case, it is the fact. Mr Garnett therefore corrected his first slip, and forgot to correct his second, which, even from his original idea of the chronology, would have been wrong.

The next point upon which I should like to say a few words is this: Several of my reviewers have put the question, "How far is Miss Clermont's testimony to be accepted ?" They say that she was old, and given to romancing. I merely reply this:

It is ridiculous, with the spectacle of an octogen-
arian premier in the full plenitude of his powers
before us, to argue that age need necessarily in any
way affect the memory or mental powers ; and, as
to the strictness of a certain *clique* of Shelleyan
idolaters, they accept Jane Clermont's testimony
when it fits in with their idolatrous conceptions,
and reject it when it does not, which is scarcely
logical. As to the tendency to romance, I do not
believe Miss Clermont was at all given to that
practice ; but, in any case, I think it will be granted
that the conversations I am now about to quote,
and also those which have already been published
in this Review, show a remarkably fair, unprejudiced,
and logical mind. When there is an object, I can
conceive a person lying, but not without an object.
I can see no reason whatever to doubt the absolute
veracity of all Miss Clermont told me. It may, no
doubt, be painful to the Shelley idolaters to be told
that the expedition to Switzerland was pre-arranged
between the Shelleys, Byron, and Claire, and they
appear to prefer to believe that "Shelley and
Mary," as they love to style their innocent little
"babes in the wood," should be led to Geneva by
the wicked sorceress, Jane Clermont, they all the
while remaining in total ignorance of her relation
to Byron ; but any man or woman of the world
would, I should be disposed to believe, think Jane
Clermont's version of the story obviously the
correct one.

I will now pass on to a conversation referring to Shelley's will, and here again I may say that in this case, reason and common-sense are distinctly on the side of Miss Clermont, and against Trelawney, who, as I have always understood, never had a good word to say for anyone except Shelley ; but I may add that I do not believe Shelley intended to leave as much as he did for his sister-in-law's exclusive use. He had made the will during Allegra's lifetime, and would have revoked the second legacy after her death had his own death not come so soon and so unexpectedly on the heels of it.

The following conversation will give her views on the subject, and also gives very excellent and, I venture to say, impartial views of both La Guiccioli and Trelawney.

Entering the drawing-room one lovely spring morning, I found Miss Clermont at her guitar— a guitar on which she was playing when Shelley was inspired to write the wonderful lines cited below—touching the strings to some old melody, and half accompanying the now feeble notes in a subdued voice, but not so subdued but that one could detect the petted singer of Florentine salons of a generation—even two generations— before. It was a perfect picture : the beautiful, thick hair falling over the shoulders, the clear-cut profile of that face, as beautiful now as ever, and the eyes which seemed lost in dreams, as those slender fingers strayed over the strings—

the same picture that inspired Shelley more than sixty years before. I stood a moment on the threshold, silent, and the servant (they all loved her) made some whispered remark of admiration to me, and then I repeated the wonderful lines:

"Thus to be lost, and thus to sink and die—
  Perchance were death indeed! Constantia, turn!
In thy dark eyes a power like light doth lie,
  Even though the sounds which were thy voice, which burn
Between thy lips, are laid to sleep;
  Within thy breath and on thy hair like odour it is yet,
And from thy touch like fire doth leap.
  Even while I write, my burning cheeks are wet;
Alas! that the torn heart can bleed and not forget."

"I have heard Constantia singing," I murmured. "I have often said I would give my life for that."

She turned round, with that wonderful smile of hers, like that of a coquette of eighteen. "Ah, it is you, is it? What a power of transfiguration you have!" she said. "Why, that was written at Marlow, dear Marlow! in—let me see—in 1817. You have heard an old woman mumbling. My voice is a ghost. I was pestered to death once by all the Florentine drawing-rooms to sing! All over Italy my voice was known, thanks to Percy. He always took such pains about my instruction in singing. But how can you say you have heard Constantia singing, now? You have only heard the thin, reedy notes of Constantia's ghost."

"Constantia is always Constantia, madame," I said. "Time cannot wither—— "

But she interrupted, laughing, "Shakespeare said that of Cleopatra in her forties. I'm afraid he would not have been equally complimentary to me in my eighties. But my forties were my best time, too. It was in my forties, and in the forties of this century, I had most money, in any case. On the old baronet's death I inherited £12,000 by Percy's will, and then I settled down in London, after having led a very unsettled life ever since Percy's death. I was until then a regular rolling-stone, wandering from place to place, all over Europe. I was a long time in Russia, in Paris—everywhere."

"Do you ever hear of Trelawney, madame?" I asked.

"I know why you ask that question," she replied, with a laugh. "Trelawney, I am told, says that Shelley did not intend to leave me more than £6000—that the second legacy was a mistake. That is nonsense; Shelley was a very good business man. It is, of course, the fashion to consider him as a being quite too ethereal to care for mundane matters—in point of fact, a kind of inspired idiot. But that is entirely a mistake. No one could be more practical than Shelley, if he liked. He had a most logical mind, and was, perhaps, the first classical scholar in Europe, of his time. No; I know nothing of Trelawney: he never was my friend, you know; and it seems to me he gives himself airs, and always has done, of knowing a great deal more of Shelley, and Byron too (but particularly of Shelley), than he has any right. 'Why, he only knew Shelley for six months."

"How he hates Byron, madame!" I said.

"Well, Byron snubbed him, you know. He said, 'Tre was an excellent fellow until he took to imitating my *Childe Harold* and *Don Juan.*' This got to Trelawney's ears, and he never forgave Byron for it. Trelawney made himself quite ridiculous when I lived in London, I remember. He absolutely lived, or in any case dined out, on the strength of his acquaintance with Byron. It was always 'Byron said this,' 'Byron did that.' I remember Thackeray takes him off rather well somewhere. I want you to write about me in due time," she said, "though not for ten years after my death. Give me that time," she added, with a smile, "to rise to another sphere altogether. It is only fair that I, who have been maligned by one set of Shelley enthusiasts, should be placed in my true light before the world ; though not a word during Sir Percy Shelley's lifetime. It seems a queer thing, by the way, that the one person whom Shelley loved best on earth, should be constantly held up to opprobrium by his idolaters."

"Well, well, madame," I replied, "we all know the reason of that, and the inspiration of Field Place! That legacy was probably unwelcome to some."

"You are right there," the lady replied. "What

an idiot I was to lose nearly all the money in that Lumley's opera-house business! I've always had a mania for music and the stage. It was through the one fancy that I first met Byron, and through the other that I lost my money. I don't know which was the greater disaster."

I laughed. "Poor Byron!" I said, "I'm longing to hear just one good word for him." And after a good deal of *badinage* between us she went on to say:

"Byron and Shelley were as far asunder as can be imagined in their estimate of women. Byron considered them as men's inferiors; he held an absolutely Oriental view of women. He was fond of saying that he did not think they had any right at the table with men, and ought to be shut up in seraglios, as they are in the East. No doubt a good deal of this was affectation, for a man who had travelled as much as he had was a rarity in those days, and he was very fond of airing his Eastern experiences, but much of it was the real expression of his feelings."

"No wonder you and he did not hit it off long together," I replied.

"No," she said; "Byron never could agree with any woman of much independence of thought."

"The Countess Guiccioli had a good deal of intellect, I suppose, had she not, madame?" I inquired.

"Oh, to a certain extent she had, but you know what Italian women are! Their education is not of a nature (and still less was it so at that time) to develop a woman's capacities⁄at all. They are just like children—rather vicious children, though. La Guiccioli was, moreover, ridiculously infatuated with Byron. That book of hers which appeared a few years ago is simply absurd! If she had been describing an angel, instead of a man who, even his greatest admirers admit, was full of blighting faults, she could not have said more."

"She became a leader of Parisian society after Byron's death, as the Marquise de Boissy, did she not, madame?"

"Yes," replied Madame Clermont; "but she was a perfect female Trelawney with her Byronic reminiscences, as Dumas describes in 'Monte Christo.' It was a standing joke when I was in Paris in the thirties and forties; people used to draw her out about Byron for the fun of the thing. La Guiccioli was always devoted to Byron's memory. An Englishwoman would have revolted at the treatment she received, but she was as faithful as a dog to him."

"Did he treat her badly, then?" I asked.

"Well, that depends upon what you call treating a woman badly; but from all I have heard he grew very tired of her latterly, and would have severed the link altogether but that he was too closely bound up with the family generally; her brother and he were great friends, and he accompanied Byron to Greece. Byron never behaved with any brutality to her, but he gave her ample cause for jealousy, and showed her in plain words, very plainly, that he was tired."

"Her book certainly struck me as absurd," I said. "As you say, if Byron had been an angel from heaven she could not have spoken of him in higher terms. I have always been told," I said, "that La Guiccioli was possessed to her last breath of a burning jealousy of you."

"I believe she was; but I never knew why, for I certainly cared nothing for Byron. I endeavoured, through Shelley, to effect a reconciliation with him on account of my child's future. Shelley went to him, and stopped some days there, when Byron and La Guiccioli shared openly the same house (to the great scandal of her countryfolk, who said 'Byron had hitherto behaved so well'), in order to try and persuade him to come to an arrangement. La Guiccioli was charmed with Shelley, as all women were, and insisted on his staying considerably longer than he had intended; but it was all to no avail. Byron was as obstinate as a mule when he once set his mind on a thing, and in this case I feel sure that he was egged on by La Guiccioli to send away my child to a convent, both out of spite, to annoy me, and also because she hated to have the child near her." And the lady's eyes filled with tears.

"Well, madame," I replied, "after all, Allegra was brought up in the same faith that you have yourself now adopted." She paid no attention to this.

"Of course," she went on, "there was a reason that Byron used as excuse for his vile conduct in thus robbing me of my child? That vile note at foot of my letter to him, which he sent on to Hoppner, and which has been since unearthed, explains it. But it was a lie."

As I made no reply, she continued, "I presume you think that there can be no smoke without fire? Well, I will tell you the whole truth now, and you may judge for yourself."

Nothing more, however, shall be written by me on this subject, so highly distasteful to me, until 1909, and not even then had not Miss Clermont requested me to give what I know to the world after the lapse of time before mentioned.

One of the most interesting things Madame Clermont told me related to the visit Byron paid to the Shelleys at Marlow in her company, in the summer of the Waterloo year. I made mention of this visit in my previous article, but the exigencies of space did not permit of my including the following most interesting and characteristic incident.

"At that time," she said, "both at the Crown Inn at Marlow and at other inns along the river, a number of French prisoners-of-war from Waterloo were confined, and at The Crown they were shut up in the stalls and loose-boxes in the stables."

" They escaped afterwards, I was glad to hear," said Madame Clermont ; and she told me the following story :

" Byron, the Shelleys, and I went to see them. Byron and Shelley, of course, as red radicals, sympathised both with the men and with their cause. Byron was a great worshipper of Bonaparte, and, though Shelley was not that, he hated the British Tory Government of the day much more than he hated Napoleon. Some of the men were sulky and surly, and we could not get a word out of them, and no wonder, for popular feeling ran very high then against France, and there were many in and about Marlow who had lost husbands and brothers and sons in the war. Therefore, the poor Frenchmen did not meet with much sympathy. People were a good deal rougher then, too, than they are now in their ways of doing things, and though they were not badly treated, the prisoners' lot was by no means what it would have been nowadays. The landlord himself, however, was very kind to them. They were all fond of him. It was a great joke with him when we were in Marlow next year and the prisoners had escaped, how one of them, the wag of the band, left a line for the innkeeper, ' Merci mille fois pour votre gracieuse hospitalité.' The jovial

48

landlord's account of the matter was very amusing.

"'I don't understand their lingo,' he said to Shelley, whom I can so well picture now, with his great gazelle-like eyes and his humorous smile (for Shelley had a good deal of humour, though it never comes out in his poetry) as he listened. 'I don't understand their lingo, and no one does hereabouts. But a nephew of mine from London came down here one day, and told me what it meant. I *did* laugh to be sure!'

"The man who sent this *billet doux*, I remember, was one of the two we paid most attention to; the other was a hard-faced veteran of a hundred Napoleonic fights, but the wag was an extremely good-looking, soldierly fellow.

"Byron said to him, 'Eh bien, mon brave, est-ce que c'était un beau combat?' and the man's eyes glistened with excitement as he shouted in a voice of thunder, 'Si c'était à refaire je le referais. Vive l'Empereur!' and one and all took up the chorus with a mighty shout which almost shook the stables.

"We caught the contagion, and both of us girls and Shelley and Byron shouted with one voice: 'Vive l'Empereur!' How ridiculous it was! The whole of England was glowing with the Waterloo triumph, Marlow no exception to the rest of the country, I can assure you. Out came the landlord, with his usually rosy, jovial face quite pale now. Had we been ordinary visitors he would probably have ordered us out of the place there and then, and we should have had to take the next coach back to London—feeling ran so high. But all the world knew Lord Byron, and though 'fallen on evil times and evil tongues,' as he was fond of saying himself—a comparison which always made me laugh, for anyone more unlike what Milton must have been it would be difficult to conceive—his name was still as that of 'a God in the land.'

"The landlord came running out. 'For Gawd's sake, my lord,' he said, 'don't shout out that d——d cry! Why, if anyone heard it in the village I'd be murdered,' and he called out, as a protest, 'Hurrah for Wellington!'

"'You d——d old rascal!' said Byron, as we all shrieked with laughter. 'Bring along four pots of ale for us, and one for each of these gentlemen of France, and we'll drink to Napoleon.'

"'It's as much as my life's worth to let you drink to Boney!' the terrified landlord exclaimed, gazing at Byron, as if the devil, tail, horns, hoofs, and all, were there, and, indeed, the ill reports of 'the wicked Lord Byron' had reached even Marlow.

"But, as was said about Byron's friend, Moore, our worthy host dearly loved a lord, and Byron, flinging him a sovereign, and seizing him with those strong arms of his, said: 'If the liquor is not here in three minutes, I'll fling you among these tigers.' And a roar of laughter came from the prisoners, for even among those soldiers of the *Grande Armée* the name of Byron was known, and 'Vive le Lor' Beeron! Vive le Lor' Beeron!' was the cry now in those stables of the Crown, where heroes were stalled worse than horses.

"The landlord arrived with two trays of pint tankards. The excitement of the men—the contagious excitement of French soldiers, brought on by the magnetism of Napoleon's name and the excitement of Byron's presence, too, his name and his fame; his unearthly beauty as he stood there, like an inspired Apollo—was indescribable. The soldiers raged like lions in their stalls, shouting alternately, 'Vive Lor' Beeron! Vive l'Empereur!' —even Napoleon was for a moment second to that other great, though mispronounced, name.

"The landlord stood by with his waiter, both with frightened faces. To call in those days 'Vive l'Empereur!' was like calling 'Hurrah for the devil!' but Byron, bidding them hand round the tankards, seized one himself. 'Now, Shelley,' he shouted, 'drink up; none of your infernal lemonade this time! Vive l'Empereur, mes braves!' he thundered, and emptied his tankard to the dregs. And a roar that must have echoed far beyond the other bank of the river sprang from the lips of each soldier, tankard in hand, 'Vive Lor' Beeron! Vive l'Empereur.'

"Byron strolled off with us afterwards (or rather limped off, I should say) with that calm, contemptuous expression on his lips which they almost always wore.

"'What a magic,' he said to me, 'that man's name has!' all oblivious of the magic of his own. 'He is one of the madmen who have made men mad by their contagion'—a remark which not long afterwards I had the pleasure of reading word for word in verse in the third canto of *Childe Harold*.

"'You are a wonderful actor,' I replied. 'What a pity that your birth prevented your taking to the stage! You would have rivalled Kean.'"

I once asked Miss Clermont a question which seemed rather to amuse her, but which seems to me to have a good deal of weight in the estimate of any man's character, and that was as to whether Byron or Shelley smoked.

"Shelley," she said, "never did. Byron at one time, when I first knew him, was a great smoker, but afterwards abandoned the habit almost altogether. On rare occasions, however, he would renew it, and when he did, it was usually to excess."

Talking about one of the haunts sacred to the memory of the two poets, Miss Clermont remarked,

"What a charming place Pisa is! Strange that it should have gone so out of fashion among the English now! Then it was the most popular English colony in Southern Europe."

"The Western Riviera is rather supplanting Italy," I said.

"Ah, but there is no place in the world like

Italy! See how all of us who have once felt its charm come back again!"

"'That Paradise of exiles, Italy!' as Shelley called it," I replied.

"Yes," she said; "nearly all who knew it in those days, who were there in our time, have gravitated back. But I am the last of all left, except Mr Severn, Keats's friend. It is significant of Italy's charm that the three greatest poets of the century should all have been there at the same time, and singular that all should have died within three years of one another.

"How strange it is," she continued: "the long-evity of all who knew the three great poets, whose own lives were so short—Keats, Shelley, and Byron —the eldest dying at six-and-thirty, Shelley at nine - and - twenty, and Keats at five - and - twenty. Trelawney, who was born the same year as Shelley, is still alive at far over eighty; I am eighty; and Peacock died a very old man; Mr Severn is more than eighty; Keats's sister, I believe, is still alive; and the false Fanny Brawne," she said, with a little laugh, "whom I knew in London, only died about 1865."

"Can you give me an introduction to Mr Severn, madame? I am anxious to see him, if I go to Rome."

"None is necessary," she replied. "He is a delightful old man, and will be only too glad to see an admirer of his beloved Keats."

"What beautiful constancy and affection that is of his! Keats died the year before Shelley, 1821, and Mr Severn keeps his memory still as bright as ever."

"Well," she continued, with a half-sigh, half-smile, "I suppose Mr Severn and I will both soon rejoin our beloved ones. 'A soul of gold,' as Shelley called him. Do you admire Keats yourself? You do not think him equal to Shelley, as some say, do you?"

I laughed. "Most certainly not! madame. Keats died far too early to give one an idea of what he might. do in mature years, and to compare him with Shelley is ridiculous, for the quantity of work he has done altogether is not a tithe of Shelley's, and what there is reminds me very much of a luxuriant but unweeded garden. Nothing can be more cloying than his earlier poetry, with his 'dear delights' and 'darling essence,' and 'cheating dove-like bosoms.' I quite agree with Byron in his contempt for all that part of 'the Mannikin's' work as he called him. But, on the other hand, the Odes are absolute perfection. Nothing can surpass the beauty of that rich golden haze of vague, sweet mystery and dream which surrounds them like a nimbus. It seems almost incredible that the same man who could write the repulsive trash that I have been speaking of, could also compose those divine lines, instinct with all the mystery and melody and glamour of old romance

—lines which alone would make a man immortal:

> Charmed magic casements, opening on the foam
> Of perilous seas in fairy lands forlorn."

"Was not that a strange presentment of his own death that Shelley had?" Miss Clermont remarked. "Was it not strange that in describing Keats's or Adonais's death, he exactly described his own?"

"That is, I always think, one of the most wonderful psychological cases in history," I replied.

"It is a strange thing," I remarked, "that that most interesting episode you have told me about Marlow and the French prisoners should never have been related before by any of the Shelley and Byron biographers."

"Oh, no, not at all!" she replied. "All the contemporaries who wrote of Byron and Shelley only came into our circle after that, in Italy. Tom Medwin and Trelawney, Hunt and the rest —Mary became far too prim and proper to write about a scene like that, living as she did in highly respectable Sussex county society. Mary always had a great respect for 'Mrs Grundy.'"

"Shelley must have tried her a good deal, then," I said. "What did she think of that poem beginning (and to whom did it allude)—

> The serpent is shut out from Paradise,
> The wounded deer must seek the herb no more
> In which its heart-cure lies"?

55

Miss Clermont did not appear altogether to care for this allusion to a *tendresse* for another Jane, and I directed my conversation to a more personal channel.

"Poor Mary!" I replied. "Fancy such a disturbing element in the house! It cannot be altogether bliss to have a lovely sister and an arch-charmeuse under the same roof with a husband who speaks the language of the gods, whose 'food is love and fame.'"

"Well, it was not my fault that men fell in love with me," she replied, with that strange half-shy, tantalising smile which irradiated her face with a flood of youth, and put it out of one's power for some minutes to realise that this was a woman of eighty.

I asked her the question if Byron had ever been in France, saying that I had always understood he had not, but that in his conversations Medwin relates an anecdote of Byron and Rogers among the catacombs in Paris.

"Absolute imagination," she replied. "Dear old Tom Medwin had the most vivid imagination; 'Bamming' he called that sort of thing, a slang word much used in those days. Byron was never in Paris in his life."

Of the Shelley *entourage*, Miss Clermont appeared to like her namesake, Jane Williams, the best. A charming woman, she said; both Shelleys were devoted to her. This lady's grief at the terrible news of the disaster which involved the death of both Shelley and her husband, Miss Clermont described to me as pitiful to witness.

"All you ladies," I remarked, "seem to have formed a kind of adoring circle around Shelley."

"Yes," she said; "Shelley had an irresistible attraction for all women; his nature was so pure and noble; the tone of his poetry whenever a woman is mentioned is of an almost unearthly purity. Instead of holding with Byron that woman is inferior to man, he looked up to woman as something higher and nobler. Many of his poems express this feeling most forcibly.

> The desire of the Moth for the Star,
> The desire of the night for the morrow,
> The devotion to something afar."

"I can imagine Shelley," I said, "almost like a pretty girl himself. I am sure that poetical epistle to Maria Gisborne is most ladylike."

She replied indignantly, "Not at all; there was no lack of manliness about Shelley. He was utterly without any sense of fear; always in the open air, yachting, or taking strong physical exertion. He was the finest walker of any man of the Byron-Shelley *clique*, and could tire out almost any of the others."

I again preserved a discreet silence. All the ladies of the clique seem to have enjoyed a passionate feeling for Shelley, and had I ventured to differ with Madame Clermont after this, I should very soon have received my *congé*.

There is one subject on which her evidence was absolutely opposed to that of any of the biographers except Mr Jeaffreson, who, with his usual acuteness and *flair*, seems to have suspected the truth. She gave me distinctly to understand that at the beginning of the Byron connection she had a pretty clearly defined idea of becoming eventually Lady Byron, and on this subject we had a great deal of conversation which cannot be reported here. Her evidence, also, was quite opposed to what I may call the "Shelley-and-Mary-babes-in-the-wood theory." She told me clearly that the Shelleys knew all about her relations to Byron, both before and during the Genevese epoch. Indeed, Miss Clermont gave me a kind of semi-romantic, semi-comical account of how the news was first brought to the Shelleys by her, before either they or Byron left England. She burst into the house one day, she said, shortly after the first interview with Byron, and exclaimed, to quote her own words: "Percy! Mary! the great Lord Byron loves me!" "Percy" was quite pleased at thus forming a kind of brother-in-law of his mighty brother bard, and I, I am sorry to say, laughed; as, indeed, did the lady when she told me the episode.

The following few particulars may be given—it is impossible to give more—of Miss Clermont's career subsequently to the deaths of Byron and Shelley. She first went to Vienna for a time, where her brother, Charles Clermont, was residing. After that she spent some time in Russia, and later on became a governess in Italy to the descendants of her old friend, Lady Mountcashel. Her position, however, in that family was quite a unique one, Lady Mountcashel's daughter always looking upon her with adoring admiration. I have many interesting particulars, both of this epoch and of her life in Russia, also in Paris (where she spent some years) and in London, where she settled on coming into Shelley's legacy, the greater part of which she lost, as explained by herself. On returning after this loss to settle finally in her beloved Florence, she took, in the first instance, a villa at S. Domenico, below Fiesole; subsequently to that she lived in Via Valfonda, and up to her death she inhabited a house in the Via Romano.

Jane Clermont's body was buried in the Municipal Cemetery at Trespidano, some four or five miles out of Florence. She had told me that she wished it to rest with that of her child Allegra, but no doubt this was not possible. It was a touching wish, and would have been a touching end to that long, chequered life had all that was mortal of Jane Clermont come to rest at last with the beloved and never-forgotten child—though the source of so much bitterness in the past—who predeceased her mother by nearly sixty years.

And now, before concluding, let me say a few words to clear up some great misconceptions that have always prevailed as to the relations of this lady and Byron. Byron did not treat her badly according to his lights. I have said this to her herself, as plainly as one can say unpleasant things to a lady, and I repeat it here. It is a peculiarity of the feminine disposition to construe slights into crimes, and to dwell and brood over matters that men would pass by unnoticed. Yet though Miss Clermont —and my readers can see it for themselves— though she obviously disliked Byron, I am bound to say she never spoke of him with injustice. Surely the Shelleyolaters should be the last to argue that he treated Jane Clermont badly, seeing that both Shelley and his wife revolved as constantly in his orbit as they possibly could, even abandoning an invitation to Florence for some months in order to continue so revolving at Pisa.

As to the "vile note" that Miss Clermont spoke of to me, the confidences she made me afterwards (but which, as I have said, cannot be published until 1909) as completely exonerated Byron as Shelley, in my opinion.

The whole history of the discordance between the two was this: Byron was a man of genius; and, like most men of genius (and a great deal more than most), he had a vast deal of the woman in his composition; while Jane Clermont was a woman to the very marrow of her bones. Need I say more? It was a question of a woman's ambition, a woman's egotism, a woman's vanity warring with a woman's ambition, a woman's egotism, a woman's vanity. I do not say that these qualities are more developed in women than in men, but they are differently developed.

A once spoiled pet of the drawing-rooms, a hot-press darling of the publishers, meets with a beautiful, fascinating, but spoiled and capricious girl—Italian in appearance and disposition (notwithstanding her strictures on Italian women), though English in depth. She wishes to use the man and his fame as a lever, and on finding that she cannot get all she wants—well, she begins to show her less amiable side; and he, equally or more spoiled, and with a fame perhaps unequalled in history, becomes furious; then love (or whatever approach to love there ever was between them) very quickly changes to intense aversion on both sides. As to Byron's subsequent conduct, it was quite in consonance with the free love tenets of his friend Shelley, who, as I have already said, never showed the slightest resentment against his leaving Jane Clermont when and how he pleased.

> "Women are but the margin of our lives
> The course goes on unheeding."

That was obviously Byron's motto. When they interfered with his life, they went to the wall: witness his wife; witness Jane Clermont; witness, even to some extent, La Guiccioli. To him, after the first heats of passion, women were pretty playthings and no more. Now, Jane Clermont's whole ambition was for glory, and display, and sensation. Amiable, generous, and dowered with a magnetic charm as she was to the last, she always felt that fiery longing to excel, to be great, to be prominent in some way or other. She had turned to Byron in youth, not from love of him, but from love of his fame, for love of sensation. She was dazzled by his glory as one is dazzled by the beams of the sun in his zenith; but her sun passed on, as the sun itself passes on over rich and poor with indifference; and then came the one love of her life—Shelley— Shelley with his soft, tender ways, and divine words; and the rest has been told. At the last came a longing for rest, and "the eternal croon of Rome" only half supplied that rest. One day I passed her pet priest as he was leaving the house, and found her much agitated.

"What is the matter, madame?" I asked, gently.

And the priest's influence seemed but slight, for she replied fiercely, though in that voice of golden accents, looking at me, a boy of twenty then, with a sort of envy, "O God, dear, to be your age! to begin life again! if I could only have another chance! I know I have it in me to be great, but I have missed it—missed it somehow!" And then, with that firm belief in a future world, this wonderful woman of many moods said, with a steady glance of those keen, piercing eyes of hers: "I shall have another chance in another world. The priest's talk is jargon. All these shows are only shadows."

My last sight of her stands pictured clear and distinct from beyond the long lapse of years—waving one white hand to me from the window, with that never-forgotten smile on her lips.

THE SECRET OF THE BYRON SEPARATION

NOTHING in the whole course of biographical literature is so replete with interest, has possessed, and
seems likely to possess, such a strange haunting
fascination as the life of Lord Byron, and no part
of that wonderful career has so baffled and perplexed the world as the epoch of his married life,
and the causes leading up to the separation.

The secret of this separation (for, notwithstanding
occasional averments to the effect that it was merely
due to the ordinary causes of incompatibility of
temper, it has been almost universally held that
there was a secret) has excited the feverish curiosity
of at least three generations, and is still exciting
the curiosity of a fourth.

It so happens that I, a man born thirty-four years
after Byron's death, am able to solve this enigma
of the century, and I am the only living man who
can do so. I shall do so now.

In two articles, entitled "Chats with Jane Clermont," which appeared in the *Nineteenth Century* at
the end of 1893 and the beginning of 1894, I reported conversations I had the privilege of obtaining
with Miss Jane Clairmont, the sister by affinity of

Mrs Shelley, shortly before her death, and throwing an entirely new light upon several aspects of Shelley and Byron literature—such as upon the first meeting between the two poets, on which point the information received by me was most striking and novel; the pre-arrangement of the Geneva meeting, and other matters which had until then perplexed all students of Shelleyana and Byroniana.

The articles met with a most generous reception from both public and Press, and undoubtedly, apart from the literary value of the revelations made by Miss Clermont to me, the sharp, incisive style in conversation of that marvel of old ladies, imparted a charm to all matter of which she treated, that same fascination which attached to her person from youth to extreme age; but in these conversations I was, as I explained, obliged to omit matter of the most vital interest—matter more interesting even than anything I included—at the special request of the lady herself.

Part, and to many the most interesting part, of that information I am about to relate in this paper —namely, the portion which gives the secret of Lady Byron's absolute determination to separate from her husband, and the reason accounting for her obstinate refusal to return to him. I am showing for the first time to the public what was the keynote of Byron's life; am plucking, as it were, the heart out of his mystery.

In breaking on this subject a silence which I

have for years observed, it cannot be said that I
am in any way committing a breach of faith to
trust. My promise to Miss Clairmont was as
follows :—Not to write in any way of the disclosures she made to me, until ten years after her
death, and then only in the event of the death
of Sir Percy Shelley taking place previously. That
promise I have more than kept, for Miss Clairmont
died in 1879, and the death of Sir Percy Shelley
took place as far back as 1890, while I did not
publish the first of my articles until November
1893. My further promise was not to publish
certain matter relating to Miss Clairmont until
thirty years after her death, and that promise I
shall also keep to the letter, as regards a great
portion of the matter, and publish nothing on the
subject until 1909, provided I am in that year
upon this planet at all ; but, after much matured
consideration, I have arrived at the conclusion that
I am at liberty to use my discretion in reference
to that part of Miss Clairmont's confidences which
relates to the Byron separation, in which, as will
presently be seen, she played the most prominent
part.

There is really no reason why all that the lady
told me should not be given to the public now,
for there is not a single living person whom such
disclosure could harm, while I have information
at my disposal regarding the celebrated Byron-
Hoppner correspondence, which completely clears

Shelley from a most atrocious charge, and fixes the responsibility, such as it was, upon the right shoulders; but still a promise is a promise, and I suppose must be kept, even if it be unreasonable. As regards the present subject, however, Miss Clairmont was certainly unaware when requesting me to make the promise, or in any case she had forgotten the fact, that the Hobhouse papers—at present under seal in the British Museum—will see the light with 1901, and the long sought-for secret will in any case be revealed then; so I am merely anticipating matters by less than six years.

I will, therefore, now give the reason for this famous separation—this separation which has given rise on one side to some of the finest poetry ever penned, in *The Dream* and elsewhere, albeit insincere and misleading at times, and at others absolutely maniacal in fury, and on the other side to the atrocious and vile calumnies repeated to Mrs Harriet Beecher Stowe, with which the author of " Uncle Tom's Cabin " disgraced her literary fame; calumnies, the offspring of a diseased, revengeful, malignant, and half-unhinged mind; calumnies, which would justify the worst that Byron ever found to say against his wife, which render it impossible to think of the woman who could utter them without a shudder, and fully to appreciate the feelings of his daughter Ada, who inherited so much of her father's temperament, on learning at last, through Colonel Wildman, successor to the lands and halls of the Byrons at Newstead, what a heritage of fame was hers, on discovering in fact that immortal father, the memory, almost the knowledge, of whom and of whose works had been sedulously kept from her.

The story is so touching and so little known that it is well worthy of relation here. A little over a year before her death, Ada, then Lady Lovelace, paid a visit to Newstead, and, on Colonel Wildman quoting a passage to her from her father's works, asked the name of the author. Colonel Wildman, in answer, pointed to the painting of Byron on the great library wall. The disclosure burst on this nervous, delicately-strung lady, of the true Byron temperament, with the force of a revelation, and for some time Lady Lovelace could hardly command herself under the shock of tender, tumultuous feeling thus aroused. Subsequently, she became a diligent student of her father's works, and of everything in any way connected with him whose memory she cherished for the remainder of her life as a sacred thing. But the thought that she had all her life been deprived of the knowledge and love of that glorious being, who had doubtless even passed away thus early from a world which he would have glorified as much by his deeds as by his words, out of bitterness of heart caused by the severance from her, while she all the while had been kept in complete ignorance both of him and of his works—this bitter thought preyed on her mind, and in a little more than a year from the time of this discovery—as it really was—of her own father, Lady Lovelace also passed away to the silent land. But during her illness she wrote to Colonel Wildman imploring him who ruled in the Byrons' place that her body might be buried by that of her father. " Yes," she said ; " let it be buried there, not where my mother can join me, but by the side of him who so loved me, and whom I was not taught to love ; and this reunion of our bodies in the grave shall be an emblem of the union of our spirits in the bosom of THE ETERNAL."

And thus were the prophetic words of Byron fulfilled to the letter.

" My daughter ! With thy name this song begun—
My daughter ! With thy name thus much shall end ;
I see thee not, I hear thee not, but none
Can be so wrapt in thee ; thou art the friend
To whom the shadows of far years extend ;
Albeit my brow thou never should'st behold,
My voice shall with thy future visions blend,
And reach unto thy heart, when mine is cold,
A token and a tone, even from thy father's mould.

Yet, though dull hate as duty should be taught,
I know that thou wilt love me ; though my name
Should be shut from thee, as a spell still fraught
With desolation, and a broken claim :
Though the grave closed between us, 'twere the same,
I know that thou wilt love me ; though to drain
My blood from out thy being were an aim,
And an attainment, all would be in vain,—
Still thou would'st love me, still that more than life retain."

And in the loss of her daughter's love, and in the passionate awakening in that daughter of love for her father, Lady Byron paid, perhaps, the price of her icy coldness and hard, unforgiving cruelty to the uttermost farthing. But the unlovely nature was only goaded on by this, goaded on from cold, implacable resentment to hellish unspeakable malice and infamy. Fortunately, the utter flagrant madness and absurdity of Lady Byron's statements to poor credulous Mrs Stowe was exposed in the *Quarterly Review* at the time the morbid and vulgar American writer gave them to the light of publicity; but it remains for me to end for ever all foolish and monstrous rumours, and to reveal the true facts to the world.

Byron himself said on several occasions that the causes of the separation were too simple to be easily discovered, and Trelawney, in his interesting " Last Days of Shelley and Byron," seems to have held the same opinion. But this is only true in a limited degree, and then only as relating to the period before the journey of Lady Byron to Kirkby Mallory —for there must have been a very powerful reason to cause a lawyer of eminence, who at first advised Lady Byron to patch up matters with her husband and return to her home, only a fortnight later to declare a reconciliation impossible. The reason for this has never yet been divulged; and it is this alone that constitutes the mystery of the Byron case. To deal with the wretched quarrels of the Byrons' married life is mere trifling with the matter. The story of the events leading up to the Byron separation has been fully told by various writers; but it is necessary here to recapitulate them in order of sequence, so that the reader may bear in mind the chronological outline of the occurrences of which I am about to treat.

For several months after the marriage all went well; but in about August or the beginning of September, quarrels broke out, and from that time until January 15th, 1816, the two led what is expressively called "a cat-and-dog life." The birth of a child in November 1815 made matters if anything rather worse, for Byron was greatly disappointed at the addition to the family circle not proving of the sex he had wished. He had taken it for granted, in the most amusing way, as is evident from his letters, that it was to be a son, and duly resented the disappointment occasioned on the presentation to him by Lady Byron of a girl. On January 15th Lady Byron travelled, then, to her parents at Kirkby Mallory, in Leicestershire, in the full persuasion that her husband was mad. Nevertheless, all arrangements had been made that he should rejoin her at Kirkby Mallory in a few weeks, and remain there until Lady Byron should be in the first stage of her progress to maternity, when she promised, no doubt, to behave better and let it be a son this time. In those days people had not the privilege of possessing an Ibsen, and were not in such dread of matters hereditary as are we of to-day. Moreover, Lady Byron and her parents also were of opinion that, by judicious treatment and humouring, Lord Byron's mind would recover its tone; and Lady Byron wrote him humorous, playful, affectionate letters, both on the day of her arrival, and on the day following, addressing him as "My dear Pippin."

Meantime, however, her ladyship was taking measures to make quite sure of the insanity of the poet; and on the very day after she wrote the second letter she received a report from Le Manu, an apothecary who had examined Byron surreptitiously (that is to say, without Byron having the slightest idea of his drift), that he could note no signs of insanity in her husband, and that his extraordinary behaviour and excitability were merely the result of over-taxing the brain, worry from his creditors, and trouble and excitement generally.

This put an entirely new complexion upon matters, so far as Lady Byron was concerned, and she vowed never again to share the same house with a man who, without the excuse of insanity, could yet treat her in the manner Byron had done; but she wished to make perfectly certain that Le Manu was right before definitely committing herself to a separation. Not a minute did Lady Byron lose in taking the necessary steps to either confirm or disprove his opinion, and on January 19th, 1816— the very day after receiving Le Manu's letter—she started for London to consult Dr Baillie, who shared twin honours with Dr Abernethy — also a Scotsman—as head of the medical profession of that day. Both physicians were noted for their brusquerie, and are referred to ironically in connection with this in *Don Juan* as "Mild Baillie" and "Soft Abernethy."

In case Dr Baillie's account of her husband should tally with that of Le Manu, Lady Byron had fully made up her mind to take the legal opinion of Doctor Lushington. For the convenience of both medical man and lawyer she had drawn out the famous statement of reasons, made such fun of afterwards by Byron, for believing him to be mad.

And here was the whole case as it then stood.

Now comes a touch of humour, one of those touches which are by no means lacking in the whole business, and, indeed, alternate with tragedy all through Byron's life. The lawyer and the doctor managed to find a pretext for visiting Byron, and were treated with the scantiest of scant politeness, indeed, only just escaped a very ignominious and forcible ejection from the house ; and not unnaturally either, for Lord Byron, of course, wholly unwitting of their purport, very properly resented the number of apparently silly, aimless, and impertinent questions asked of him. He alludes to this in a letter written years afterwards, and the visit is also the subject of the sprightly verses, so broadly humorous

73

that one can never read them without laughing,
in *Don Juan.*

> "But Inez called some druggists and physicians,
> And tried to prove her loving lord was mad;
> But as he had some lucid intermissions,
> She next decided he was only bad—
> Yet when they asked her for her depositions,
> No sort of explanation could be had,
> Save that her duty both to man and God
> Required this conduct—which seemed very odd."

Byron's demeanour during this interview was,
notwithstanding the short work he made of his
extraordinary interviewers, of a nature to render it
quite certain that he was not mad, and the lawyer
and the doctor returning to Lady Byron with this
intelligence, quite confirmatory, as has been seen,
of what she had already been told, that lady betook
herself at once to Doctor Lushington to ask his
opinion as to whether a separation was practicable.
Doctor Lushington replied that a judicial separation
could, no doubt, be obtained, but that the circumstances were not such as to warrant him in advising
his client to incur all the scandal and publicity of
this course, and the consequent sacrifice of domestic
happiness which might still quite well be hers—with
a little give and take, bear and forbear on both sides;
and he recommended that Lord Byron should be
seriously remonstrated with, both by her and his
own relatives (both Captain George Byron and
Augusta, Mrs Leigh, his sister, were entirely on the
wife's side), and that then Lady Byron should return

to her husband, and they were—as the story-books say—"to live happy ever afterwards." Such was the sensible and paternal advice of this excellent counsel. Lady Byron was half-disposed to act upon it. Her simple old father was very wroth, and vowed that his daughter ought never to return to a sane man who had treated her so; but his daughter, as history and biography have only too well proved, had a decided will of her own. Moreover, she was, after all, sincerely attached to her husband, and detested the horrors, scandal, and publicity of a judicial separation. She returned with her father to Leicestershire, and spent a fortnight there in wretched indecision; when something occurred which led her again to seek the advice of Doctor Lushington, and this time he advised her precisely the reverse of what he had previously counselled.

Before, as has been seen, he had strongly recommended a re-union, but now he said a re-union was impossible. More than this, Sir Samuel Romilly, the counsel retained by Lord Byron for the defence, on learning that his wife was determined to sue for a separation, threw up his brief, and returned the money, on hearing the additional facts submitted to Doctor Lushington, and declared that he would take neither part nor lot against Lady Byron, who, he considered, was entitled to the relief afforded by separation.

What was the reason for this change of front?

We all know the generous disposition of the lights of the law ; chivalrous to Quixotism ; and how apt, as a class, they are to throw over briefs and return money, if their sensitive souls be not satisfied of the justice of a cause ; but in this case the reason must have been very powerful. What was it ? All manner of answers—answers that might almost be counted by the thousand—have been made to this question. Hints of unnameable vices, of unnameable crimes, even, have been freely offered. Murder, even, has been suggested ; but nothing possible—or impossible, I should say—has been left unsuggested for the last seventy - nine years, except the right solution, which I am about to give. The most noted, of course, of the solutions has been the equally hideous and absurd story of Mrs Harriet Beecher Stowe, above alluded to ; but that has been amply demolished already, as I have said ; and, even if true, it would be fully as disgraceful to the woman who could tell it to silly Mrs Stowe, as if absolutely false—as it is. For the woman who could live for years on terms of intimacy, and even affection, with another of her sex, of whom she could believe such a thing possible, would be as unspeakable as the woman who could invent such a tale.

To deal with the true reason for this most celebrated of all connubial severances, I must transport myself back long years ago now—to the last years of the decade before last. I must transport myself to a quaint, dark, old Florentine drawing-room ;

and a vague, longing pain—a longing for I scarce
know what—steals over me now.

Nicht irdisch is des Thorens Trank noch Speise.

How well I can picture the scene! It stands
more clearly than my life of yesterday before me
now—when I learned first this secret of Byron.

I see a lady—old, I suppose ; but she never seemed
old to me, with that wondrous youth which seemed to
baffle time, lighting up the mobile, Southern face—
for, as I always told her, she was in appearance, as in
disposition, an Italian—an Italian with the deep soul
of an Englishwoman—I see her, as she speaks in that
low, sweet, musical voice, with which time had dealt
as gently as with all else concerning her. The only
thing on which the relentless destroyer had set his
mark was on the hair, and there he had only touched
in play, for the locks were as luxuriant as in the
old golden days by Lake Leman, when the burning
words of passion were poured into that ear like a
white sea-shell from the lips of a poet whose strains
have thrilled the world as the world has never been
thrilled before or since—words such as no woman
on earth can hear now. The locks had been changed
from glossy black to a glistening white, every whit
as lovely—that was all. For the lady was Jane
Clairmont,—Jane Clairmont, loved in the old time
by Byron, loved passionately by sunny Thames
stretches, and blue Genevan waters, and deep Alpine
recesses, until the cold wind of discord blew upon

that love, the sudden extinction of which has ever been another unsolved mystery, partly explained by me already, but to be more fully explained now. It was Jane Clairmont—beloved by Shelley to his latest breath—who spoke thus now to a boy of twenty, seated on a little ottoman at her feet, and listening with all the enthusiastic interest and ardour of youth to the wonderful new things this wondrous survival of the past had to tell, this still beautiful lady of the witch-like charm, upon whose lips the lips of Shelley and Byron had rested. How entranced the boy was at all this flood of remembrance, gazing up to that sad, poetic face, with the coquettish, wilful curve of the lips, and the enchantress smile which showed upon them from time to time, taking away in an instant sixty years from her eighty of life. How strange to think that I was that boy! That all the fate reserved for him was to develop into the present writer, with youth and illusions, which alone make life worth living, gone for ever.

Eheu fugaces! Posthume, posthume Labuntur anni.

"What brought on the Byron separation, dear?" the lady said in response to a question I had put to her. "Well, as Byron said, the causes of the quarrel were very simple, too simple to be easily found out. The two quarrelled like cat and dog."

"Yes, madame," I replied; "but I mean, what made Lady Byron decide she would never go back to her husband, and led to the extraordinary change of opinion on the counsel's part?"

"Oh, Byron was a very bad man, you know!" Miss Clairmont replied. "No doubt, other reasons occurred which led Lady Byron to take a stronger view of the case than she had first done."

I somehow felt I was being trifled with, and, looking up, I noticed that mysterious *demi-sourire* on the lady's lips, and I smiled back in return. A sudden thought flashed across me as I reflected despairingly that evidently Miss Clairmont was not disposed to be communicative, and I expressed the thought.

"Byron himself attributed his married misfortunes and the mischief made between him and Lady Byron to a namesake of yours, madame. Was she any relative? I have often wondered as to the coincidence of names. And yet, if she were, it is strange that none of the Byronic writers have said anything on the subject."

"Certainly she was — a connection by marriage with an uncle of mine, I should say; I am thankful to say there was no nearer relation."

"Byron's verses to her fame in a sketch are certainly not complimentary," I remarked.

"That is the most ferocious thing he ever wrote," Miss Clairmont replied; "but I must say the old wretch fully deserved anything that could be said against her. She was the cause of all the trouble, and it was all through hatred of me."

I started at these words, feeling that now I was on the brink of a great disclosure, if I could only induce this reticent lady to speak.

"All through hatred of you, madame!" I said. "But what had you to do with it?" I asked, innocently.

She smiled again, with that part-playful, part-wicked, part contemptuous smile of hers, like the smile of a spoiled beauty, radiant in the insolence and pride of young loveliness — the smile which must have worked such deadly effect on the heart of Byron long years back, and replied:

"Well, I suppose I was the immediate cause of Lady Byron's resolve."

At last! At last I was about to hear the solution of the great mystery!

"Tell me, madame," I said; "I will be very good, and say nothing for as long as ever you like."

And having made me give the promise before referred to, and holding one of my hands in that delicately-moulded hand of hers with the snowy fingers of Constantia, as I sat on the ottoman at her feet, she proceeded in that gentle, flute-like voice, with the perfectly modulated cadence, showing the once-renowned singer, to tell me the following strange story. After that, other disclosures throwing the most vivid light upon the characters both of Byron and Shelley were related to me, and we sat together until the sweet Italian dusk, and then the divine Italian night, populous with stars shining over dome and cupola and ancient mansion of fair Florence, surprised us.

"I have told you already," the lady said, "of how I met Byron first, and of how the whole world was then dazzled by his glory—dazzled by it almost as much as by that of Napoleon—I with the rest. I, a beautiful girl—for I was beautiful then—I can say it now without vanity," she added.

"You may say it of yourself now, without vanity, madame," I protested; but, with an imperious wave of the hand, she silenced me and went on:

"I was a romantic girl. *Espiègle* they used to call me—that word has died out now, has it not?" she asked here.

"There are no Constantias belonging to this age, madame, to turn the heads of the world's greatest men, and the word has fallen out of use."

She smiled, and continued:

"Mrs Clairmont, who, as I have said, was married to my uncle, found out my connection with Byron in this way. She had all her life been a meddlesome busybody and mischief-maker; had hated Byron from the very first, and had determined from the day of his marriage to do him an injury, and upset any chances of married happiness the two might have. She hated me, too, for I was a girl with a sharp tongue, and rather prone to be sarcastic, and to make fun of people."

"In those respects I think you still unchanged, madame," I said.

She laughed, and replied: "Well, if so, it does credit to my powers of endurance, for I am sure I have gone through enough; but, in any case, such was my disposition then, and my charming aunt hated me accordingly. When Byron's connection with Drury Lane Theatre began she thought her opportunity come at last. She used to hang about the stage doors of the theatres, and actually went the length of employing spies with a view to finding out if he cultivated any relations with the actresses. Nothing, however, could she discover; and then a really fiendish idea occurred to her. On several of her visits to our house the question as to what I should do in life was discussed. It was clearly necessary for me to do something, as my father's—I mean Mr Godwin's—means were very small, and all that I could see or had any inclination for in the way of a career was the stage—either the opera or the drama. Mrs Clairmont, hearing of this, and of my idea of calling upon Lord Byron at Drury Lane, saw at once an opportunity of gratifying her spite in case things turned out as they did — and she estimated Byron's character correctly—— "

The lady hesitated a little at this juncture, and I ventured to interrupt, remarking: "It would appear to me, madame, that you and Byron were ideally suited to one another. You seem to me to have just the mixture of poetic responsiveness and quick, sarcastic observation and satirical power that

82

Byron should have adored. Your very appearance is that of a Byron heroine."

Miss Clairmont laughed. "*Was*, you flatterer, *was*, perhaps," she said. "Ah yes; he did adore me once, passionately no doubt for a time! But Byron grew to hate me; and I returned his hate with interest, for he was the curse of my life, though now I can look back through the past without bitterness."

"And yet, madame," I urged, "those enchanting days at Leman among the forests and the mountains; those days spent with the deathless poets, the remembrance of those golden days of .passion and all the glamour of romance which must have so intoxicated both souls; even a life would be well lost for such remembrances."

"A pretty background," she replied dreamily, as though her thoughts were far away in some other world; "but life has been so long, so wearisome, after all," she said; then—as if suddenly awaking from a reverie—"a woman's life is not intended merely to serve as part of a *mise en scène* for the tableaux of a poet's career, however great he may be; my life was worth as much as his." She said this with much bitterness. "Do you, too, think, so young as you are, with him who said:

> Women are but the margins of our lives :
> The course flows on unheeded?"

she asked, looking at me keenly.

83

I thought it better to turn temporarily the conversation into a more jocose channel, for I could see that these recollections were becoming very painful to her.

"Heaven forbid, madame," I said. "I should like them to take up all the text, for they are all we know of angels."

"And the margin? What would you have as margin?" she asked.

"The margin should be made up of dreams," I replied.

She laughed merrily, then, with that low, melodious laugh that used to bring the tears to my eyes when I thought of how her innate fortitude and courage had survived in that clear, sweet laugh all misfortune and disappointment.

"Why do you laugh, madame?" I asked. "That is cruel of you, when I have just been comparing your sex to the angelic hosts."

"It was a picture that came across my mind," she said, "of you in the future as an old Pasha with 'a garden of fair women,' as Tennyson calls them, around you, with an opium pipe between your lips, enjoying 'the margin,'" she replied. "The fair women, I suppose, you would like to gaze at you in adoration the while until you came back from dreamland. Such, no doubt, is a true representation of your sex's idea of woman's proper place."

"Oh, madame, how can you say that?" I remonstrated. "Think of Petrarch, and the years and years of his Platonic adoration for the cold Laura."

"Oh, pray do not instance that nincompoop," replied this wilful lady. "There never existed a man for whom I have more contempt. Sighing, and suing, and billing and cooing all those years to a woman with ten children, who, after all, would not as much as allow him to kiss her hand."

"Oh, as to the limits," I replied, "you must remember we only have Petrarch's word for that. Petrarch was doubtless *un monsieur comme il faut*, and would not tell tales out of school. Besides, is it not of the very essence of Platonic love that it is a system of progression?

A hand may first, and then a lip, be kissed,"

I quoted.

"You wicked boy, I will not allow you to talk scandal of the immaculate Laura, though, in my opinion of that lady, I must say I am at one with Byron. Do you remember his quotation? —

If Petrarch's Laura had been Petrarch's wife,
Would he have written sonnets all his life?

"Probably the claims of her little Petrarchs, if she had presented him with as many as she did, in fact, to her *légitime*, would have been a distinct impediment to the muse, and Petrarch rightly pre- ferred the chaste security of Platonic love."

"Doubtless, doubtless, madame," I replied, and quoted:

> " The noblest kind of love is love Platonical,
> To end with or begin with ; the next grand
> Is that which may be christened love canonical, ·
> Because the clergy take the thing in hand.
> The next sort to be mentioned in our chronicle,
> As flourishing in every Christian land,
> Is when chaste matrons to their other ties
> Add what may be termed marriage in disguise."

This interlude of chat and laughter having diverted Miss Clairmont's mind from melancholy thoughts which had previously beset her, she resumed her narration.

" Mrs Clairmont," she said, " found out by means of her own, all about myself and Byron, and told, in the first instance, Lady Noel about it, and *she* told Lady Byron. Yet it was through this woman that I first met Byron."

" I thought that *you* called on him at Drury Lane," I said.

" So I did," the lady replied ; " but if it had not been for Mrs Clairmont I should never have paid that visit. She introduced Lady Noel, Lady Byron's mother, to my stepfather, Godwin, and a kind of literary set in which I mixed, and some of the set Lady Noel used to visit, and occasionally met at the houses of her friends. I was one of these, and I was first presented to Lady Noel and to Lord and Lady Byron at a reception by Mrs Clairmont, who had accompanied Lady Noel there. She was a special companion of Lady Noel, and used to accompany both her and Lady Byron everywhere.

Byron paid me great attention on that occasion, and that gave me the idea of calling on him with a view to obtaining a part, as he had been good enough to talk a great deal about how I seemed to him to be born to be a great actress, and so on. He never made the slightest effort to do anything for me on the stage after I had called on him. Such was the worth of Byron's promises."

"I suppose he grudged such a gem to the vulgar interests of the world, madame," I replied.

"A pretty way of putting it," Miss Clairmont replied. "But allow me to tell you, my young friend, what I had occasion to tell Byron — that talk is remarkably cheap, and that, as the Spaniards say, it butters no parsnips."

"Did you fall in love with him at first sight, madame?" I asked.

"Oh, don't ask such leading questions," Claire replied, laughing heartily this time. "You ought to be a cross-examining counsel. I suppose I did, though; he was a gloriously handsome man at that time, with a soft, insinuating, irresistible manner, and a voice like music itself. And a fame—and a fame—but I have told you of that. Why, the women, the greatest women of the time, too, were even brought to him to be presented, instead of his being presented to them—as if he were a king. If I fell in love, however," she added, "in another year I had completely fallen out of it, knowing his disposition better. Well," she went on, "I have told you of my visit to Byron at the theatre, and about the ideas of free love in which I had been brought up by Mr Godwin, and which were exemplified by Shelley and Mary."

Miss Clairmont gave me distinctly to understand that though she had met Lord Byron in the first instance during 1815, the connection between them was not suspected until after the departure of Lady Byron to Kirkby Mallory; but, before—and this contains the secret of the whole matter — Lady Byron returned to town to consult Dr Lushington for the second time. Moore, in his life of Lord Byron, says that Lady Byron had no cause for offence on grounds of infidelity until after the period of the separation, and Moore would be right as regards what was actually known if by the separation he meant the departure of Lady Byron for Leicestershire; but, as has been seen, there was no intention of separating on her part when she first left London; indeed, she was continually expecting her husband to join her, and had written him warm and affectionate letters. Undoubtedly, however, Lady Byron could adduce this *liaison* as further evidence against her husband when she consulted Dr Lushington for the second time. And not only had she been told of the *liaison* by Mrs Clairmont while at Kirkby Mallory, but, on her second visit to town, an incident took place which put the fact beyond all manner of doubt.

I prefer to relate this culminating point of the story in my own words from a natural feeling of delicacy towards my old friend. The disclosures made by Mrs Clairmont, through hellish malice and snake-like, poisonous hate to Lady Byron, appalled that lady with their suddenness and brutality, and she hastened up to London to see Dr Lushington; but it was her first intention to confront Byron and ask for the truth or falsehood of Mrs Clairmont's assertion from his own lips. She called at the house in Piccadilly, but heard that he had gone to John Murray, the publisher's, in Albemarle Street. To Albemarle Street Lady Byron accordingly proceeded. Lord Byron was not at Mr Murray's; but, on issuing from the shop, she saw him entering another house in the same street with an extremely pretty, piquante brunette, whom she well knew to be Jane Clairmont.

Lady Byron, with her usual self-command, told her coachman to drive on to her solicitor's, who advised inquiries to be instituted to make security doubly sure. It was ascertained, therefore, that Lord Byron had, for some short time past, been in the habit of making use of these rooms to meet Miss Clairmont. Byron pleaded, in a letter to his wife, which may probably be found among the Hobhouse papers, that this intimacy did not begin until after Lady Byron had left him to his own devices; but Mrs Clairmont, with fiendish malignity, suggested that it had gone on for some months, and, having in view Byron's conduct towards his wife, this otherwise additional and overwhelming fact induced Dr Lushington to pronounce the opinion he did, and Sir Samuel Romilly to throw up his brief for the defence; a course he probably adopted, less from any feeling of chivalry, than from a distaste to expose himself to part of the storm of obloquy which had already begun to rage against Byron.

There, then, is the secret of the Byron separation. The publication of the Hobhouse papers will probably prove that I am in the right in giving it as a reason; and even if I had not, as I have, absolute confidence in what Miss Clairmont told me, everything tends to show that it is the true one. Among other proofs I may mention the date of Allegra's birth; for had that child been the result of an intercourse only began in Geneva —as so many silly Byronists and Shelleyans seem to wish to have been the case and to resent the other view (though what it can matter to them I must say I fail to see)—that child would have been prematurely born by, in any case, a month, which she certainly was not; not to mention the gross improbability of a man like Byron living upon terms of Platonic affection for months with a girl of Jane Clairmont's views. However, I am quite content to accept Miss Clairmont's word. Her interest (if there were any question of interest in the matter at all) would have rather been to lead

me to believe that she did not yield to Byron's
solicitations until meeting him again in Geneva,
and thus give herself the benefit of posing as coy
and reluctant. But she was far too honest for
that, and told me plainly that neither she nor
the Shelleys saw anything wrong in the connection
(as, indeed, the Shelleys, in view of their own
connection, could hardly do), that they were all
three apostles of free love.

The reasons why this explanation has always
been withheld are very obvious. In the first place,
Mrs Clairmont had prevailed upon both Lady Noel
and Lady Byron to keep her name out of the
matter, in order that she might not be exposed
to Godwin and the others of the family as a relation capable of playing so detestable a part; and
Byron's intimate relationship with the Shelleys
gave another good reason for his silence as to the
affair, while Moore and the contemporary Byronian
biographers have glossed over the Jane Clairmont
episodes altogether as much as possible, out of consideration for the feelings of Godwin, a brother man
of letters. I must say, however, that it seems to
me very strange that no writers on Byron should
have suspected the relationship between the two
Clairmonts. One would have thought that the
mere coincidence of name (by no means a common
one in this country) would have led to research
into the question of their possible connection.
Possibly the various manners of spelling the name

may have prevented this; and the elder and highly objectionable lady seems occasionally — notably in Lady Blessington's "Memoirs"—to have been known as Mrs Charlemont.

With the question of the orthography of the name I have dealt in a number of the *Times* during the November of 1893.

Besides clearing up the Byron separation mystery, another result of the light I am enabled thus to throw on Byron's life explains the inveterate antipathy which grew up between himself and Jane Clairmont. The reasons for this I have, to some extent, explained elsewhere; but the fact that Miss Clairmont was really the cause of the separation from his wife, and especially from his child, whom he so passionately longed to rejoin, and the way in which, through the chatter of the English colony at Geneva, the matter leaked out, despite Byron's precautions, both by action at the time, and in writing subsequently, to keep the *liaison* secret, induced him, in that irrational feminine manner, which was a great defect in the poet's character, to regard the once passionately admired beauty as an enemy, and an obstacle to the re-union with his wife and re-establishment in England.

Consequently, before the Shelleys and Claire had left Geneva, a breach had taken place between the latter and Byron. No doubt, had Claire taken more pains to conciliate this man of the impulsive, self-willed disposition, the *liaison* might have lasted much longer; for in disposition she far more resembled Byron than La Guiccioli, than whom in beauty she was vastly superior also. But the very likeness of their dispositions led to the premature disunion. I remember once mentioning my astonishment to Miss Clairmont that Byron could leave a woman of her charms for the foolish, credulous, dumpy Guiccioli, and remain with the latter so long, and she replied : " La Guiccioli endured things from Byron I should have disdained to endure from a demi-god."

Before closing this article, the information given in another letter to the *Times*, which I now quote, will probably be of interest to the reader. A good many people have been under the impression that Miss Clairmont's body was buried by that of her daughter Allegra, in Harrow Churchyard, whither Byron, with great trouble, transported Allegra's remains. But this is quite a mistake, as my letter shows :

" *January 5th*, 1894.

" CHATS WITH JANE CLAIRMONT.

"SIR,—As you so kindly allowed me to make use of a portion of your valuable space once before, when dealing with some friendly reviews of my first article on above subject, which took some exception to my orthography of the lady's name, perhaps I may once more venture and ask permission to add some highly interesting information

93

which our esteemed Consul-General in Florence, Sir D. E. Colnaghi, has had the great kindness to procure for me.

"There has always been a mystery as to where the body of Jane Clairmont was buried, and I was led to believe that it was at Trespiano, in the Municipal Cemetery, although the lady herself had expressed to me personally an ardent and pathetic wish that her mortal resting-place should be that of her daughter Allegra, who died in 1821.

"Sir D. E. Colnaghi has, however, after great trouble, for which I cannot be grateful enough to him, ascertained that the grave is in the cemetery of S. Maria, in the Commune of Bagno à Ripoli, about three and a half miles from Florence.

"There is a marble slab on the grave, and under the names, surmounted by a cross, are the words :

> " 'She passed her life in sufferings,
>   Expiating not only her faults, but
>   Also her virtues.'

No more touching, no truer, words were ever writ. But this information throws a new light on the much-disputed nomenclature of Jane Clairmont. Shelleyan and Byronian authorities have held Constantia to be a mere *nom de fantaisie*; but apparently this is not the case, for all four names to which I alluded in my first letter to the leading journal — *viz.* Clara, Mary, Constantia, Jane—appear on the tomb.—I am, Sir, yours faithfully,

"WILLIAM GRAHAM."

During her last years Miss Clairmont shared her home with a niece, by name Paula Clairmont; and this lady, with whom I fancy she was latterly not on the best of terms, met with a terrible death some ten years ago by a fall into a glacier.

In conclusion, I would merely remark that, though

it must at least be admitted that I have in this article cleared up the great Byron mystery, it may be said by some that I have still left unexplained the reason of Lady Byron's absolute refusal to be reconciled to Byron. But in that I maintain there is no mystery whatever. Byron worshipper as I am (and I confess that the very name of the man and the fire of his verse affect me even now with the same mesmerism which "thrilled the boys and killed the girls" when the century was young, while I detest the very name of Lady Byron), still, I must be just, and I must admit that Byron's conduct as regards his wife after the separation, though intelligible in a man of his passionate vehemence and incontinence of emotion, was indefensible. The witty verses quoted from *Don Juan, apropos* of Inez — who, of course, was merely Lady Byron transported to Spain — were not precisely of a nature to induce more affectionate and forgiving feelings towards him any more than were the terrible incantation in *Manfred* and *The Dream*, in the latter of which, out of malice against his wife, he led the whole world to believe he had never loved her at all. At intervals — from the separation until the Blessington episode, which induced gentler feelings—Byron girded constantly against Lady Byron, whom, nevertheless, he really loved in his way, and passionately desired to rejoin eventually on account of his child. The long array of successive mistresses, of whom, of course, kind

95

friends brought her the story, did not tend to mend matters. Jane Clairmont was the reason of the separation, but was no impediment to the re-union, except, perhaps, as she herself told Byron in a letter which is extant, that Lady Byron might draw a moral from his treatment of Allegra as to his desirability for assuming parental duties towards his legitimate daughter. As a matter of fact, however, his treatment of Allegra, if not of the mother, was very creditable, and it is extremely improbable that this weighed at all. There is no mystery whatever as regards the continuance of the separation ; the only strange thing would have been had Lady Byron consented to pardon during his life, as long as it lasted. If she had, she would have acted as not one woman in a thousand would have done. In 1823, as I have said, he began to assume a very conciliatory tone ; and, no doubt, had Byron returned from Greece as liberator and king, as undoubtedly, had he lived to attend the Salona Congress, would have been the case, he would have been welcomed with affectionate love by his wife, and with a passionate enthusiasm by his country, throwing even the enthusiasm that greeted the author of *Childe Harold* into the shade. It is Lady Byron's conduct after his death, not during his life, that I so strongly condemn and execrate.

But her calumnies and all other foolish inventions and lies I have now set at rest ; and perhaps my countrymen and his will feel that some gratitude is due to me for one thing at least that I have done— to have swept away these foul vapours, and to have placed the character and career of—after Shakespeare in the opinion of many—our greatest poet, in its true light before the world.

KEATS AND SEVERN

AMONG the memorable friendships of literature, there is one which shines out pre-eminently from all the others, even as that of Orestes and Pylades, of Damon and Pythias, among the friendships of old time. Indeed, the only friendship I can think of to equal this in full completeness is that of our dramatic *dioscuri*, Beaumont and Fletcher. But that alliance in life and art of two souls, "twain halves of a perfect heart"; this remembrance gleaming through the mists of ages with serene glow of friendship rendered deathless, falls yet far short in charm of the marvellous attraction that the mere cursory recollection of the love of Severn for Keats must exercise on all with any appreciation for devotion unswerving, fidelity unchangeable, womanly tenderness, and love passing the love of woman. Through Keats, Severn became immortal; but was the former's crown of poetry, were the lyre on his tomb, and the deathless laurels which only came after death; was the tribute of song to his memory and for his grave —by his mighty contemporary, Shelley—were all these greater distinctions than this, the glory of his friend, so to have enshrined his memory in the hearts of the nation with the greatest literature on earth, that, whenever the mention of one of its greatest poets is made, cheeks must flush and eyes must moisten at the story of heroic devotion; that whenever the name of Adonais is spoken, the name of Severn must find place beside it—a name that Shelley could regret he had not known of earlier? He would then have enshrined him in the deathless name-roll of *Adonais*. "But Mr Severn," said he, "can dispense with reward from such 'stuff as dreams are made of.' His conduct is a golden augury of the success of his future career. May the unextinguished spirit of his illustrious friend animate his pencil and plead against oblivion for his name."

Shortly before the death of Mr Severn, during a journey across Italy, I called upon him. The trio of revolutionary poets of the early days of the century possessed a peculiar attraction for me, and my interviews with the last survival but one of the Byron and Shelley circles only whetted my desire to learn more. And in Keats there was an undiscovered world; a world not so full, perhaps, of moving incident and romance stranger than any romance in fiction, but possessing equal attraction in the vague, unfulfilled, though splendid promise of a life cut short so early; that weirdness and mystery of so young yet so splendidly full a life, so perfectly self-orbed and developed a nature, which gave rise to those memorable words of our greatest woman poet:

"But Keats's soul, the man who never stepped
In gradual progress like another man,
But turning grandly on his central self
Insphered himself in twenty perfect years,
And died not young (the life of a long life
Distilled to a mere drop, falling like a tear
Upon the world's cold cheek to make it burn
For ever) ; by that strong excepted soul,
I count it strange and hard to understand
That nearly all young poets should write old."

And scarcely less than my desire to hear of Keats was my longing to behold, in flesh and blood, this glorious friend of the "inheritor of unfulfilled renown."

It was a handsome old man, though a very old man indeed, who approached me on entering that room in Scala Dante, and after cordially greeting me, remarked, with a cheery laugh, "You are probably only just in time to see me ; in a very short time now I am due to join my friend Keats and the rest of my generation." And indeed it was true enough, for he only lived for a few months longer than Miss Clairmont, whom I had just left ; Trelawney, the last of the band, living into 1881. "Well, well, I have had enough of it, for I am nearer ninety than eighty now, and it is time to say *Nunc dimittis*. For us artists, too, there is no place to live or die in like Rome."

"You appear much attached to Rome, Mr Severn," I said. "Has the memory of your friend been the reason of your living so much there ?"

"Partly, no doubt, but not altogether," replied he. "Rome has all my life possessed a profound attraction for me; and since I led Keats there, I have spent nearly all my time in Rome. I was British Consul from 1861 to 1872, you know. Rome is like a human being to me: what I love most in the world. I knew well how Keats would revel in the art treasures, and I hoped sanguinely that the climate would cure his complaint, or in any case protract his life long enough to allow of the accomplishment of greater work than he had ever done."

"Could that have ever been, Mr Severn?" I questioned. "Could anything surpass 'The Odes'?"

"Perhaps not," was the reply. "But I hoped for more from him than five perfect odes; and perhaps they, and some others of his briefer poems, are the only portions of his poetry that can be properly described as 'perfect.' I took the same pride in Keats," he added, with that sweet, amiable smile of his, "that I would have done in a young painter who promised great genius but wanted development."

"How many painters," I thought to myself, "would endeavour thus to push a contemporary because 'they promised great genius'? Would they not rather do all in their power to keep them back in this world of envy, hatred, malice, and all un-charitableness?"

"I think Keats's great attraction for me," Mr

Severn went on, "was his appreciation and sympathy for my own art, and this grew and grew with the years. He showed a decided talent for painting himself; but, of course, poetry was paramount to everything with him. But I may at least claim the hearty thanks of the lovers of the sister art for one thing: you would have never possessed the *Ode to a Grecian Urn* but for me. He saw the urn with me, and it was a favourite subject of conversation with us."

"The lovers of literature have even more cause than that to reverence your name, Mr Severn," I said. "That name shall be spoken with reverence ages hence, 'In states unborn, and accents yet unknown.'"

The old man's eyes softened. "I was only a man who loved his friend," he replied, simply.

I asked him if Keats appreciated music as much as painting.

"Keats appreciated all that was beautiful," he replied; "but he had no educated feeling for music."

"His feeling for music, I suppose," said I, "was something like that of the Duke in *Twelfth Night*:

> That strain again; it had a dying fall:
> Oh! it came o'er my ear like the sweet South
> That breathes upon a bank of violets,
> Stealing and giving odour.

The same love that he had for watching the daisies

and buttercups growing in the meadows, or the trees in the forest, or the rustling of the wind through the leaves, or the taste of cool, delicious wine on the palate, or the sense of beauty however conveyed—not the sense that could have ever made him, appreciate a Palestrina or a Wagner. One regrets so bitterly that he could not have lived longer," I continued; "but perhaps, after all, had he done so, he might have done no better work. These decrees of the Great Unknown Power are doubtless for the best. His life seemed so rounded and complete, as Mrs Browning has so beautifully said. No doubt, no more was intended or possible in this life; and Shelley's gorgeous pictures in *Adonais* of the after-world are true, after all."

"There was certainly no possibility of further life in this world," replied his old comrade. "I did not know it then; but I know it now. The recent publication of his letters to Fanny Brawne puts a complexion on the case I never realised before. Keats suffered from a disease that I never suspected, which must have gnawed at his springs of life. I often wondered why the clear air of Rome worked no improvement. No; it was not the review in *The Quarterly* (though the idea gave rise to a clever couplet by Byron, and an immortal poem by Shelley) which caused his death. But I do not believe with others that it was merely his disease cither, for I think that life might long have been prolonged with care. Tubercles were not developed before leaving England, and the doctors held out hopes; but I saw at the time there was something which I could not then understand, fighting against my care and labour. That man died of love, if ever man died of love."

I smiled. "You may well add, 'if ever man died of love,' Mr Severn," I said. "Shakespeare has said:

> Men have died and worms have eaten them:
> But not for love."

"What Shakespeare puts into the mouth of a character need not necessarily mean Shakespeare's own belief," Mr Severn replied. "But I grant that such deaths are infrequent. Here was certainly one, though. The physical disease was there, no doubt, but life might have been long protracted but for that."

"Did Keats never allude to this cankerworm in any way to you?" I asked.

"Not a word ever passed his lips," he replied. "Perhaps it might have been far better had it done so; it would have eased his mind, and, knowing the Brawnes as I did, I could have given him good advice. Poor Keats made terrible mistakes in the one love affair to which his heart was given. How could he have imagined that a girl like that, flighty and flirty, could keep pace and time with the fiery poetical ideas, the feverish jealousy, the restless suspicions, and the supersensuous, supersensitive feelings he describes sometimes in prose equal to his poetry? Bah! It was Lord and Lady Byron, Shelley and Harriett Westbrook over again. What riddles men are to all but themselves, and in another way to themselves also! What riddles! what riddles!" And the old man, resting his chin on his hand, gazed out of the window into the depths of that blue Italian sky—that same sky that Keats had so longed to see, and saw only in time to die beneath its canopy—and a chill hand seemed to press upon my heart as the terrible apparent aimlessness, the awful loneliness of life, realised themselves with a sudden flash. Here was this glorious old fellow, who had been faithful unto death; had been the last and only one by his immortal friend's death-bed; had smoothed down those Hyperion locks in the death agony, but had been astray, astray till now, as to the causes of that death; and now the close-guarded secret, which he had never even suspected, was revealed just as his time to go had come.

Mr Severn had, of course, known of Keats's affection for and semi-engagement to Miss Brawne; but, as he said, he had always deemed him of too broad a nature to become the victim of a hopeless passion for *one*. And, indeed, the whole tone of Keats's writing, both in poetry and prose, tends to support this view. But what a mystery is human nature! This man with the light, jocund, frank temperament when in health, with the fierce, suspicious temperament when suffering from the ravages of his cruel disease, but in either case a man apparently without a secret, had passed out of the world, had passed out of it while in the arms of his best and truest friend, and had borne this secret with him, only to be revealed sixty years afterwards. Whether it should have been ever revealed is, of course, as a matter of good taste and feeling, extremely questionable, though, no doubt, in the interests of English literature, it was well. Lord Houghton more than suspected Keats's secret; but it was the letters, published shortly before Mr Severn's death, which proved the matter. Until then, more or less, the old tale which Byron has rendered popular by a gibe and a rhyme, too good to abandon, even although Keats's friend had told him of its falsity, still held sway:

"Jack Keats, who was killed off by one critique,
    Just as he really promised something great
    If not intelligible—without Greek—
    Contrived to talk about the gods of late,
    Much as they might have been supposed to speak.
    Poor fellow! His was an untoward fate.
'Tis strange the mind, that very fiery particle,
Should let itself be snuffed out by an article."

These lines have rung in the ears of the thousands of his readers, whose number has gone on increasing year by year, and have done more to prejudice opinion against Keats than anything else. The very ardour for fame was caused, in great measure, by the poet's wish, not only to distinguish himself, but to amass money, and thus render himself more a match for the girl to whom his whole heart was given, but whom, with money lost and health gone, there seemed no prospect of making his, save by a bold bid for fame—fame which even that pretty, light-headed, middle-class girl could appreciate. It is true, therefore, that the cruel article affected him, but not from inordinate vanity or sensitiveness, as Byron supposed, but because it rang, as he thought, the death-knell of his love hopes.

In reference to this same article, I may here clear up a point which has been much mooted. The authorship thereof has been ascribed alike to Brougham, to Lockhart, and to Gifford, the editor of *The Quarterly*, himself. But I have the best reasons for believing, from my conversations with Mr Severn, and from other evidence, that it was really written by Croker—who was never even suspected ; Croker, who seems to have been the *bête noir* of everyone of liberal tendencies connected with literature, both at that time and during the next generation ; Croker, the vilified of Macaulay, the very Hounhymn of Benjamin Disraeli, and the Sir Pandarus of Troy, of Vanity Fair, otherwise Wenham : and yet Croker, the highly-esteemed of the Duke of Wellington, and all the Tory Government and aristocracy of the day. He has, in all conscience, enough to bear on his shoulders as it is, if the views of him taken by the three great writers just mentioned in any way approach to the truth. But I am afraid I must add the responsibility for the Keats article, such as it is, to his burden. It was indeed natural enough that Croker, the arch-Conservative of the old crusted pattern, should detest this friend of republican Leigh Hunt; that this worshipper of the Regent, and contributor to *The Quarterly*, as conservative in literature as in politics, should view with abhorrence a young upstart, who was, at the same time, a kind of poetical pupil of the man who passed two years in prison for lampooning the Regent, and who set all the old school of poetry at ridicule and defiance. If even Byron, the Radical, who, romancist as he was, could yet profess to follow, in theory at least, the old school of writing ; if he could speak of " flaying the mannikin alive," then how much more Croker? Keats rushed upon his fate, as regards the Tory reviews, when he wrote that poem to Hunt, on Hunt's release from prison.

On the occasion of a second conversation with Mr Severn, I asked him as to the friendship between Keats and Shelley.

"Well, you can scarcely call it friendship," he said ; "they hardly knew one another well enough for that. Shelley was, of course, a passionate admirer of Keats ; and through *Adonais*, and that splendid fragment of Shelley on Keats's lines for his own tomb :

Here lieth one whose name was writ on water.
But ere the breath that could erase it blew,
Death in remorse for that fell slaughter—
Death, the immortalising winter flew
Athwart the stream : time's printless torrent grew
A scroll of crystal, blazoning the name
Of Adonais.

—through that verse and *Adonais*, the names of
Keats and Shelley have come down to posterity
coupled together. But Keats, on his side, by no
means reciprocated the enthusiasm of Shelley.
This has been alluded to before, but the true cause
has, I feel sure, not been arrived at. It has been
put down to Keats's independence of character,
rendering him suspicious and impatient of Shelley's
superior social position ; and, no doubt, this may
have had something to do with Keats's hesitation
to accept Shelley's offers of hospitality, but it
certainly would not have affected his literary
estimate ; for no man could better separate *the
man*, in his adventitious circumstances, from the
artist than Keats. He was a warm admirer of
Byron, for instance, notwithstanding his own
poetic bent lay in quite another direction, and
notwithstanding Byron's violent abuse of him.
No ; it was another feeling than this altogether.
The two natures were essentially dissimilar. Keats
was an artist pure and simple. Shelley was far
more than this : he was, or thought he was, a
reformer, bitter and uncompromising, of the whole
existing social order, burning with a fierce

proselytising ardour; while Keats was perfectly content with the world as it was, only desiring calm and leisure and health to cultivate his beloved art, to which he gave his whole soul; and more than once he found fault with Shelley for not being, as he said, 'more of an artist.' Both were drunk with the sense of beauty; but Shelley was far more universal, and imbued with a far deeper spiritual sense. In their very virtues the two could hardly be expected to sympathise; both were kind-hearted and generous to a degree, but Keats's sympathy for ordinary human nature had nothing to say to Shelley's transcendental longings and poems and Archimedean endeavours. Moreover, Keats had that great qualifying element, a sense of humour, which was entirely lacking in Shelley."

Here, however, I must differ with Mr Severn. As has been clearly proved by many anecdotes which have come down to us about him, and as was clearly stated to me by Miss Clairmont—as I have mentioned in an article on the subject recently—Shelley had a decided sense of humour, though of a somewhat elfish and uncanny stamp, a good deal resembling Byron's. In fact, I have personally come to the conclusion that Shelley was as much indebted to Byron for his humour, as Byron to Shelley for his metaphysics. The ridiculous incident which so amused Keats, as his letter to Leigh Hunt proves—the incident of the Hampstead coach and the old lady and Hunt:

"For God's sake let us sit upon the ground
And tell strange stories of the death of kings,"

is sufficient proof of his sense of humour; and
there are many other such proofs. No doubt, as
Mr Severn himself said, had the two lived longer,
they would have grown to appreciate each other
fully. Shelley's wonderful amiability, unselfishness,
and that perfect tact of his, born of those qualities,
would have disabused Keats of any mistrust.

"In the case of Miss Brawne," Mr Severn remarked, "it was a case of 'pride cometh before a
fall' with poor Keats, evidently, for just before
meeting her he had written to his brother, saying
how his love for beauty in the abstract prevented
his fixing his affections upon the individual.
Shelley was, after all, far more general in this
respect, notwithstanding his spirituality."

"Ein uebersinnlicher Freier?" I said, interroga-
tively, with a smile.

"Well, I don't quite say that," Mr Severn replied, smiling also, "and I am quite sure you
would not have dared to say it to Miss Clairmont;
but somehow I cannot conceive of Shelley fixing
his affections on any one woman for long. He
was clearly altogether so much less of the world,
so much less flesh and blood than dear Keats."

"I understand what you mean." I replied.
"Shelley looked upon the world and all the
universe as merely the outer shell of a vast spiritual
organism, and when he found himself tricked by

the outer semblance he wearied and sought elsewhere—for whatever his search might be. To him
everything—the wind, the sea, the waving forest,
the beauty of woman, the charm of art, was an
expression of something beyond, something that
could never be revealed until

> The painted veil which those who live
> Call life

was lifted. Keats, too, has some of this spiritual
sense, but not nearly so deeply grafted. For him
the things which make the beauty of life, for
which, as he again and again says, he alone lived,
are enough in themselves. He has no wish to lift
the 'painted veil,' no curiosity for a world beyond;
when he speaks of death it is only as some kind
of voluptuous rest or swoon. Shelley is by far the
greater poet, Mr Severn."

But the staunch old man would not give in to
this. "Keats died much younger," he said. "Had
he lived for the remaining five years, which would
have brought him to Shelley's age at his death,
who knows what he might have done?"

"I do not believe he would have done better
work," I said. "I believe Mrs Browning was
right. Of course, I have no right to speak to one
who knew him intimately; but his mission seems
to me to have been complete, his life rounded to
fulfilment, his work over. Had Shelley been able
to accomplish his desire of 'keeping Keats's body

warm, and teaching his mind Greek and Spanish,'
Keats would, no doubt, have produced poems of
a more correctly classical nature. We should have
had no new Hyperion, perhaps, nor Odes."

It may be interesting, perhaps, at this point to
note that on my asking Mr Severn what he considered the finest work in poetry that Keats had
done, he cited the glorious sonnet to Ailsa Craig.
I told him that, in my estimation, and probably
in that of most, the Odes held a higher place.
But who can blame his preference? for the sonnet
to Ailsa Craig is a magnificent piece of work. I
can remember the old man's face brightening up
with animation as he repeated those lines, instinct
with the roar and mighty music and majesty of
the sea and winds:

" Hearken thou craggy ocean pyramid ;
 Give answer from thy voice, the sea-fowls' screams.
 When were thy shoulders mantled in huge streams?
 When from the sun was thy broad forehead hid?
 How long is 't since the mighty power bid
 Thee heave to airy sleep from fathom dreams ;
 Sleep in the lap of thunder or sunbeams ;
 Or when grey clouds are thy cold coverlid ?
 Thou answer'st not; for thou art dead asleep.
 Thy life is but two dead eternities—
 The last in air, the former in the deep ;
 First with the whales, last with the eagle skies.
 Drowned wast thou till an earthquake made thee steep :
 Another cannot wake thy giant size."

Mr Severn held that many of Keats's letters con-
tained quite as fine poetry as any of his actual

poetical works, in support of which he read me that exquisitely painful, that exquisitely beautiful last letter of Keats to Fanny Brawne before leaving England—a heart-broken and desparing outburst, which, though in prose form, contains remarkably fine poetry:—

"Shakespeare always sums up matters in the most sovereign manner. Hamlet's heart was full of such misery as mine when he said to Ophelia, 'Go to a nunnery, go, go!' Indeed, I should like to give up the matter at once. I should like to die. I am sickened with the brute world which you are smiling with. I hate men, and women more. I see nothing but clouds for the future. Wherever I may be next winter, in Italy or nowhere, Brown will be living near you. I see no prospect of any rest. Suppose me in Rome: I should there see you as in a magic glass, going to and from town at all hours. I wish you could infuse a little con-fidence of human nature into my heart. I cannot muster any: the world is too brutal for me. I am glad there is such a thing as the grave. I am sure I shall never have any rest till I get there. At any rate, I will indulge myself by never seeing any more, Dilke, or Brown, or any of their friends. I wish that I were either in your arms, full of faith, or that a thunderbolt would strike me. God bless you.—J. K."

"What wasted energy!" I thought, "all this is! How much more to the purpose it would have been had he sent the lady a box of chocolate-creams, or a dozen of gloves just half a size too small. How much more either would have been appreciated."

"He might have lived to old age, but for that fatal passion," the old man murmured sadly, with tears in his eyes. "And all the time I was by his bedside day and night, impotent, and wondering what the sudden collapse could mean. How could Mrs Brawne and her daughter ever expect him to come back with that iron in his soul? You must excuse me," he said, passing his hand rapidly over his eyes, "you must excuse me if I am stupid and moody. I seem to see Keats and Fanny Brawne as they were sixty years ago."

For full ten minutes we sat in silence. Neither seemed to wish for words. Our silence was more eloquent. As for me, I was overpowered and dazzled with the glory of this undying love, which shrivelled up, like parchment in a furnace, any materialistic ideas I might have had:

"And like a man in wrath, the heart
Stood up and answered, 'I have felt.'"

"Stupid and moody!" The man who could bear a love like this for sixty years—sixty years the eternal city—eternal, though ever changing—had held this eternal love to which time was nothing. And he—he, I think, was back in the days when Keats and Brown, Dilke, Shelley, and himself, were young fellows dreaming dreams of future greatness, as they strolled beneath the trees, and among the furze on Hampstead Heath—then, not the Hampstead of now—or listening to the nightingales by Highgate Meadows, or floating on the upper reaches of the river, on golden summer days. Thinking, perhaps, how he won the prize which took him to Rome; of the glorious future that seemed stretched before him in a golden haze; thinking, perhaps, of Shelley's praises; thinking, certainly, of two figures that I felt by some magnetic affinity were pictured clear before both of us then : the figure of a young poet with deep, inward eyes, deep as the sea or sky, and gleaming with a light not of this world ; a beautiful face already just touched with the hectic bloom betokening the approach of a disease which never spares, and those eyes fixed with an earnest, soul-devouring gaze upon his companion, a gaze the intensity of which deepened the flush on that delicate cheek, as the lips quivered with pain at some gay, thoughtless speech of the other figure in our reverie—a beautiful girl of the true English type, clean cut and lissom, with a delicate hawk-like face ; a girl straight as a reed, with a willowy form, and bright eyes glistening with fun and malice —that malice of girlhood.

Beautiful, too, she was, with that *beauté du diable* of eighteen, which was indeed too truly the *la beauté du diable* in this case. And the girl laughs at some passionate words of the poet, words which, perhaps,

if they had been writ, would have added another
garland to his fame; a girl to flirt with young under-
graduates and cool-headed and clever men of the
world, like the poet's friend, Brown, but not to
understand the longings of a poet striving to realise
the ideal of universal loveliness, and panting for the
unattained. To such as her his poems and his
longings and his burning words would be so much
eccentricity—madness, no more. The poems might
sound nice, but they did not sound so nice as
a rattling valse tune, and a present of them
would not be one tithe as nice as a new ball-
dress. And the poet himself, very nice too, when
he was sensible; and he made love so beautifully.
But he had such strange fits. After all, a smart
young stockbroker like Brown would be much more
satisfactory. And it was on this shrine that one
of the triumvirate of the young century—one whose
name will only die when the memory of English
poetry passes away, " like a tale that is told "—offered
his love; it was at this shrine that the love, that
the life, of " Adonais " was offered up.

Mr Severn pressed my hand kindly at last, and
we awoke from our reverie. He looked at me
a moment, and with that keen, intuitive power of
comprehension which must have always rendered
him unsurpassed as a friend, he said, " You have been
thinking with me; I feel it. Our thoughts have
been travelling on the same track. Time has been
annihilated. How strange to think he died in my

arms when I was twenty-seven! And yet he cannot be dead. How could a dead thing influence one like this?"

"He lives! he wakes! 'tis Death is dead, not he!" I replied; and thinking of the scene now, the lines of the great poet who left us the year before last came irresistibly to my mind, though they had not seen the light then — lines which express exactly what must have been in that devoted friend's mind then:

"Peace! let it be! for I loved him and love him for ever:
The dead are not dead, but alive."

Mr Severn and I conversed for hours, on the occasion of my visit, about Keats as a poet, and Mr Severn proved that if he himself had taken to that line he would have been as fine a critic as an artist—indeed, probably finer; for, notwithstanding the marvellous promise he evinced in early years, he somehow never quite attained to that position which was prophesied for him by Shelley, and, in fact, by everyone who knew him in his early days. The death of his beloved Keats, perhaps, damped his ambition to excel. In any case, the only works of any importance he executed since 1820, when he gained the Gold Medal and the Three Years' Travelling Studentship for his Una and Redcross Knight in the *Cave of Despair*, which enabled him to proceed to Rome with Keats, are very limited in number. There are a number of portraits, including many of Keats, and one of Baron Bunsen, but the principal other works are *Cordelia Watching by the Bed of Lear*, *The Roman Beggar*, *The Fountain*, *Rienzi*, and an altar-piece for the Church of St Paul's at Rome. Mr Severn and I talked, as I say, exhaustively about Keats, both personally and poetically, but there is no further need of Keats's criticism. Keats has been weighed in the balance by the keenest experts and not found wanting, and his niche is a little lower than those of Byron and Shelley. I have been able to do something towards preserving the personal memory of a man which has fallen under the shadow of a greater name, and such a noble memory should in itself never meet with death. With this and the enshrinement of the views of his best friend on Keats, I am content, and have no desire to enter the arena of critics and appraisers.

A few words only before closing. I asked Mr Severn as to whether the reproach of "cockney," as applied to Keats, had any foundation, and he told me not the slightest as regards him personally. Keats came of a good stock, of lowly birth, of course, but still of most superior mental gifts, and the atrocious cockneyisms and conceits in his earlier poems were altogether traceable to the influence of Hunt, an influence which he was, in his last years, rapidly throwing off. Keats was wonderfully without literary vanity, which is surprising in view of the admiration he received in his own clique.

He never took offence at honest criticism, and would tear up poems in the most surprisingly ready way —a practice which it is to be regretted is not more frequently adopted among our latter-day poets.

I will now add the following corrections as to mistakes in dates (astonishing enough) which have been made by several well-known writers on Keats.

Several writers of Keatsiana follow that most inaccurate of writers, most unreliable of Cockneys, Leigh Hunt, so humorously "taken off," a generation or so later, by Dickens, who speaks of Keats as having just completed his twenty-fourth year when he died, and others seem to have a partiality for anticipating his decease, and placing it in December 1820. As a matter of fact, Keats was born on 31st October 1795, and died in Rome 23rd February 1821, so he had completed his twenty-fifth (and not his twenty-fourth) year by nearly four months at the time of his death.

I now conclude this article, in which I have endeavoured to the best of my ability to bring home to my readers the personality of the last but two of the survivors into this generation of the contemporaries and companions of the three great early century poets —Byron, Shelley, and Keats. Mr Severn died in the same year as Miss Clairmont. The last survivor of the Byron-Shelley clique was Trelawney, who died in 1881, and the last of the Keats circle was the younger sister of the poet, Fanny Keats, who became Madame Los Llanos, and survived until as late as 1889. There is no one now left to tell us in living accents of these glorious poets; and it is with a feeling of sadness that one looks back upon them, for now that their only equal, the late Laureate, who stepped in so easily to fill their place, and filled it so nobly for fifty years, has gone, who is there to succeed him? We have some great poets among us still, but their fine poetry belongs to a past generation, and even then, it could not be compared to that of those morning stars of the young century. And as for the younger generation —*Voces et preterea nihil.*

W. H. WHITE AND CO. LTD.
RIVERSIDE PRESS, EDINBURGH

LEONARD SMITHERS & CO.'S
List of Publications

NEW ART BOOKS

Ben Ionson ; His Volpone ; or, the Foxe.

EDITION DE LUXE of Ben Jonson's most celebrated Comedy, printed in demy quarto size on art paper, and embellished with a Cover Design, a Frontispiece in Line, and five Initial Letters decorative and illustrative, reproduced in half-tone from Pencil Drawings by AUBREY BEARDSLEY, together with a Critical Essay on the Author of the play by Vincent O'Sullivan, and an Eulogy of the Artist by Robert Ross. Bound in blue cloth, with an elaborate Original Design in gold by Mr Beardsley. Price 7s. 6d. net ; edition limited to 1000 copies.

ONE HUNDRED COPIES ONLY ON JAPANESE VELLUM, bound in pure English vellum, with gilt design. Price Two Guineas net. These copies contain a duplicate set of the plates, beautifully printed in photogravure in the same size as the Original Pencil Drawings.

Six Drawings Illustrating THEOPHILE GAUTIER's Romance "Mademoiselle de Maupin," by Aubrey Beardsley.

Folio size, in a Portfolio of grey cloth and boards. Fifty copies only of this Series of Six Photogravures (being reproductions of an uncompleted set of Illustrations by the late Aubrey Beardsley to "Mademoiselle de Maupin") have been printed, at the price of Two Guineas net.

A Book of Fifty Drawings by AUBREY BEARDSLEY. With an Iconography of the Artist's work by Aymer Vallance.

Demy 4to, bound in scarlet cloth extra, with cover design by Mr Beardsley. Edition (500 copies) printed on imitation Japanese vellum, 10s. 6d. net; 50 copies, printed on Imperial Japanese vellum, Two Guineas net. Illustrated Prospectus gratis and post free on application.

This Album of Drawings comprises, in addition to several hitherto unpublished designs, a selection by Mr Beardsley of his most important published work ("Morte Darthur," "Salome," "Rape of the Lock," "Yellow Book," "Savoy," etc.). The volume is of additional interest to the Artist's many admirers from the fact that the plates are in most cases reproduced from the original drawings, with due regard to their size and technique, thus preserving many delicate features which have been, to a great extent, lost by the treatment the drawings received on their first publication. The frontispiece is a reproduction of a photograph of Mr Beardsley.

Application for the Japanese Vellum Edition should be made at once, as the edition is almost exhausted. The Japanese Vellum Editions of "The Rape of the Lock" and of "The Pierrot of the Minute" are quite out of print, and selling at an advanced price.

A Second Book of Fifty Drawings
by AUBREY BEARDSLEY.

Demy quarto, bound in scarlet cloth, extra, with cover design by Mr Beardsley. Edition (1000 copies) printed on art paper, 10s. 6d. net. Fifty copies printed on Imperial Japanese vellum, Two Guineas net. [*Ready in December* 1898.

This Album of Drawings will contain about Twenty hitherto unpublished designs, in addition to a selection of the artist's best published work.

The Savoy. Edited by ARTHUR
SYMONS.

The complete set of "The Savoy," bound in three volumes, in artistic blue cloth cases, with original cover design by Mr Aubrey Beardsley, is offered for sale at ONE GUINEA net.

ART CONTENTS—Among the Art Contents are a notable series of Forty-two Drawings by Aubrey Beardsley; three Lithographs by Charles H. Shannon, and one by T. R. Way; Caricatures by Max Beerbohm; Views in London by Joseph Pennell; Unpublished Illustrations to Dante's Divine Comedy, by William Blake; and examples of the work of Botticelli, Whistler, D. G. Rossetti, Eisen, Charles Conder, Louis Oury, W. Rothenstein, F. Sandys, Jacques E. Blanche, J. Lemmen, W. T. Horton, Ph. Caresme, Albert Sterner, W. Sickert, Mrs P. Dearmer, Phil May, W. B. Macdougall, A. K. Womrath, Fred Hyland, etc. etc.

LITERARY CONTENTS—Among the contributors of Prose and Verse are W. B. Yeats, Edmund Gosse, George Moore, G. Bernard Shaw, John Gray, Frederick Wedmore, Paul Verlaine, Max Beerbohm, Fiona Macleod, Vincent O'Sullivan, Clara Savile Clarke, Bliss Carman, Emile Verhaeren, Edward Carpenter, Havelock Ellis, Selwyn Image, Humphrey James, Joseph Conrad, Theodore Wratislaw, Ernest Dowson, Rudolf Dircks, Mathilde Blind, Cesare Lombroso, Leila Macdonald, Hubert Crackanthorpe, Edgar Prestage, George Morley, Ford Maddox Hueffer,

Osman Edwards, Stéphane Mallarmé, Antonio Ferreira, R. M.-Wierzbinski, Joseph Pennell, Ernest Rhys, Edith M. Thomas, O. G. Destrée, Sarojini Chattopâdhyây, Lionel Johnson, Jean Moréas, Gabriel Gillett, O. Shakespear, Aubrey Beardsley, Arthur Symons, etc. etc.

These three volumes, profusely illustrated, and luxuriously printed, in crown 4to, on fine paper, at the Chiswick Press, present a most interesting record of the work done in 1896 by the "New School" of English writers and artists.

The Rape of the Lock. By ALEXANDER POPE. Illustrated by AUBREY BEARDSLEY.

Edition de Luxe of the above famous Poem, printed at the Chiswick Press, in crown 4to size, on old-style paper, illustrated with nine elaborate drawings by Mr AUBREY BEARDSLEY, and bound in specially designed cloth cover. Limited edition, price 10s. 6d. net. Twenty-five copies on Japanese vellum, at Two Guineas net.
[Large Paper Edition out of print.

The Rape of the Lock. Bijou Edition,

consisting of 1000 copies on art paper and 50 copies on Japanese vellum, in demy 16mo. The publisher thinks that the reduction in size of the plates in this edition has in no way injured their attractiveness or brilliancy; a new cover design was furnished by Mr Beardsley, and the cover design to the 1896 Edition is reproduced on the third page of this volume. The volume is bound in a specially designed scarlet cloth cover. Price 4s. net. Fifty copies printed on Japanese vellum, price One Guinea net.

The Pierrot of the Minute. A

Dramatic Phantasy by ERNEST DOWSON. Illustrated with Frontispiece, Initial Letter, Vignette, and Cul-de-Lampe by AUBREY BEARDSLEY.

Three Hundred Copies, crown 4to, price 7s. 6d. net.
[Large Paper Edition out of print.
Mr Beardsley's designs in this volume are amongst the most charming which have come from his pen.

Fourteen Drawings Illustrating

EDWARD FITZGERALD's translation of the "Rubaiyat of Omar Khayyam," by GILBERT JAMES.

Demy quarto, bound in scarlet cloth, extra. Limited edition, printed on art paper, 7s. 6d. net. *[Ready in December 1898.*

Caricatures of Twenty-five Gentlemen

By MAX BEERBOHM. With an Introduction by L. RAVEN-HILL.

Edition of 500 copies, printed on art paper, crown 4to, bound in blue cloth extra, with special cover design by the Artist. Price 10s. 6d. net.

CONTENTS.—The Prince of Wales, The Earl of Rosebery, Paderewski, Henry Labouchere, M.P., A. W. Pinero, Richard le Gallienne, A. J. Balfour, M.P., Frank Harris, Lord William Nevill, Rudyard Kipling, Sir W. Vernon Harcourt, M.P., Aubrey Beardsley, Robert S. Hichens, Henry Chaplin, M.P., Henry Harland, George Alexander, The Marquis of Queensberry, The Warden of Merton, Joseph Chamberlain, M.P., George Bernard Shaw, Sir George Lewis, George Moore, The Marquis of Granby, Beerbohm Tree, The Duke of Cambridge.

The Novels of Honoré de Balzac.

The First Issue consists of " SCENES OF PARISIAN LIFE." In Eleven Volumes.

THE SCENES OF PARISIAN LIFE comprise—" Splendours and Miseries," " Cousin Bette," " Cousin Pons," " History of the Thirteen," " César Birotteau," " The Civil Service," " House of Nucingen," and " The Petty Bourgeois," and are now for the first time COMPLETELY translated into English by competent hands, and illustrated with a series of eighty-eight etchings after drawings by celebrated Parisian book-illustrators—viz. G. Bussière, G. Cain, Dubouchet, L. E. Fournier, A. Lynch, A. Robaudi, and M. Vidal. The volumes are handsomely printed on deckle-edged paper, demy 8vo, and bound in cloth extra. Price £4, 4s. per set of eleven volumes.

There is a special *Edition de Luxe*, printed on Imperial Japanese vellum, with the etchings in two states Before and After Remarqués. Price £8, 8s. per set.

This first series will be followed at a brief interval by the remaining works of Balzac, and subscriptions may, if desired, be given for the entire " Comédie Humaine."

" It is impossible to enter on a detailed criticism of Balzac's novels. In them he scales every height and sounds every depth of human character,—from the purity of the mysterious Seraphitus-Seraphita, cold and strange, like the peaks of her northern Alps, to the loathsome sins of the Marneffes whose deeds should find no calendar but that of hell. In the great divisions of his Comédie, the scenes of private and of public life, of the provinces and of the city, in the philosophic studies, and in the Contes Drôlatiques, Balzac has built up a work of art which answers to a mediæval cathedral. There are subterranean places, haunted by the Vautrins and ' Filles aux yeux d'or '; there are the seats of the money-changers, where the Nucingens sit at the receipt of custom ; there is the broad platform of every-day life, where the journalists intrigue, where love is sold for hire, where splendours and miseries abound, where the peasants cheat their lords, where women betray their husbands ;

there are the shrines where pious ladies pass saintly days ; there are the dizzy heights of thought and rapture, whence falls a ray from the supernatural light of Swedenborg ; there are the lustful and hideous grotesques of the Contes Drôlatiques. Through all swells, like the organ-tone, the ground-note and mingled murmur of Parisian life. The qualities of Balzac are his extraordinary range of knowledge, observation, sympathy, his steadfast determination to draw every line and shadow of his subject, his keen analysis of character and conduct. Balzac holds a more distinct and supreme place in French fiction than perhaps any English author does in the same field of art."—*Encyclopædia Britannica.*

La Fille aux Yeux d'Or. Translated

from the French of Honoré de Balzac by ERNEST DOWSON, and Illustrated with six designs by CHARLES CONDER.

Five Hundred Copies, royal 8vo size, bound in blue cloth extra, with gilt cover design. Price 12s. 6d. net.

An attempt has been made to produce an edition worthy of the reputation of one of the most famous productions of Balzac. Attention is directed to the method pursued in producing the illustrations—viz. wood engraving, which, it is hoped, will be a welcome change from the cheap photographic processes now so much in vogue.

Les Liaisons Dangereuses (Dangerous

Entanglements) ; or, Letters collected in a Private Society, and published for the instruction of others. By CHODERLOS DE LACLOS. Translated by Ernest Dowson, and illustrated by Monnet, Fragonard Fils, and Gérard.

To render this edition of " Les Liaisons Dangereuses " worthy of its fame as one of the *chefs d'œuvre* of Literature, it is illustrated with fine photogravure reproductions of the whole of the 15 charming designs of Monnet, Fragonard Fils, and Gérard, which appeared in the much-coveted French Edition of 1796, and which are full of that inexpressible grace and beauty inseparable from the work of these masters of French Art of the eighteenth century.

This translation of " Les Liaisons Dangereuses " is complete in two volumes, demy 8vo, containing upwards of 580 closely-printed pages, and the impression of the book is strictly limited to 360 copies, each numbered. The book is choicely printed on good paper, and bound in blue cloth extra. Price, to subscribers only, Two Guineas net.

La Chartreuse de Parme.

By STENDHAL (Henri Beyle). Now first translated by E. P. ROBINS.

Illustrated with thirty-two Etchings by G. Mercier, from designs by N. Foulquier, and Portrait of the Author. Now ready in three volumes, post 8vo, printed on Dickinson's antique paper, artistic binding, £1, 1s. net. Special Edition, printed on Van Gelder's hand-made paper, £2, 2s. net; and Edition de Luxe, printed on Imperial Japanese vellum, with Etchings in two states, one pulled on Japanese vellum, and one on pure vellum, £5, 5s. net.

The Publishers feel that the production of the first English translation of this famous novel, one of the masterpieces of French literature of the present century, needs very little in the way of introduction or explanation. The Author, a contemporary of Balzac—who described him as "an immense genius," and pronounced "La Chartreuse de Parme" his masterpiece—though not generally recognised at his true value during his lifetime, could say with a confidence which has justified itself: "I shall be understood in 1880"; for, as Bourget has justly observed: "We now speak casually of Balzac and Stendhal as we speak of Hugo and Lamartine, Ingres and Delacroix."

Red and Black. (Le Rouge et le
Noir.) By STENDHAL. Now first translated by E. P. Robins. With Frontispieces by Dubouchet, etched by Gustave Mercier. Two volumes, post 8vo. Price 7s. 6d. net.

WORKS BY ARTHUR SYMONS

London Nights.

Second Edition, revised, with a New Preface. Large post 8vo. Price 6s. net. A few Large Paper copies of the First Edition remain. Price One Guinea net.

Silhouettes.

Second Edition, revised and enlarged. A few Large Paper copies remain. Price One Guinea net. Large post 8vo. Price 5s. net.

Amoris Victima : A Poem.

I. Amoris Victima. II. Amoris Exsul. III. Amor Triumphans. IV. Mundi Victima. Large post 8vo. Price 6s. net.

Studies in Two Literatures.

Large post 8vo. Price 6s. net.

WORKS BY VINCENT O'SULLIVAN

A Book of Bargains. Stories of the
Weird and Fantastic. With Frontispiece designed
by Aubrey Beardsley. Crown 8vo. Price 4s. net.

The Houses of Sin : A Book of
Poems. Large post 8vo. Price 5s. net.

The Green Window : A Book of
Essays. Large post 8vo. Price 3s. 6d. net.

[*Ready in December* 1898.

The Ballad of Reading Gaol. By
C. 3. 3. Large post 8vo. Price 2s. 6d. net.

The Importance of being Earnest.
A Play by the Author of "Lady Windermere's
Fan." Pott quarto. Price 7s. 6d. net. 50 Large
Paper copies, price One Guinea net.

[*Ready in January* 1899.

Verses. By ERNEST DOWSON
Three Hundred Small Paper copies on hand-made paper,
Imperial 16mo, bound in Japanese vellum, with cover design by
AUBREY BEARDSLEY, at 6s. net ; and 30 Large Paper copies,
printed on Japanese vellum, at One Guinea net. Printed at the
Chiswick Press.

Orchids : Poems by THEODORE
WRATISLAW.

Two Hundred and Fifty Small Paper copies on foolscap 8vo,
deckle-edged paper, bound in cream-coloured art linen, at 5s.
net ; and 10 copies, printed on Japanese vellum, at One Guinea
net. Printed at the Chiswick Press.

I

Nocturnes and Pastorals : Poems

by A. BERNARD MIALL. Large post 8vo. Price
5s. net.

The only reliable Work on the subject in the English Language.

The Life and Times of Madame

du Barry. By ROBERT B. DOUGLAS.

A limited edition in one volume, with a Portrait of Madame du
Barry finely engraved upon wood, 394 pages, demy 8vo, bound in
blue cloth, with armorial cover design by AUBREY BEARDSLEY,
at 16s. net.

" Mr Douglas has produced a volume every line of which I read with keen
interest. It is a singularly vivid and life-like picture of what life in the old French
Court was like : and the portrait of the central figure of the book is very clear and
very telling."—Mr T. P. O'CONNOR in the *Weekly Sun.*

"At a time when the book-market is flooded with translations of forgotten and
apocryphal French Memoirs, it is something to meet with a newly-published
biography of a French celebrity which is what it pretends to be . . . and is a
book of fascinating interest."—*Daily News.*

The Reign of Terror. A Collection

of Authentic Narratives of the horrors committed
by the Revolutionary Government of France under
Marat and Robespierre. Written by eye-witnesses
of the scenes. Translated from the French.
Interspersed with biographical notices of prominent
characters, and curious anecdotes illustrative of a
period without its parallel in history. In two
volumes. With two Frontispieces : being photogravure portraits of the Princesse de Lamballe and
M. de Beaumarchais.

"The Reign of Terror" is complete in two volumes, demy
8vo, containing together 530 closely-printed pages. The volumes
are illustrated with portrait frontispieces of the Princesse de
Lamballe and M. de Beaumarchais, reproduced in photogravure
from rare and well-executed contemporary engravings. The book
is choicely printed on fine paper, and bound in blue cloth extra.
Price 16s. net.

The Souvenirs of Jean Léonard,

Coiffeur to Queen Marie Antoinette. Written by
himself. Now for the first time translated into

English. With Historical and Explanatory Notes by Alexander Teixeira de Mattos.

This translation of "The Souvenirs of Léonard" is complete in two volumes, demy 8vo, containing together 702 closely-printed pages. The volumes are illustrated with portrait frontispieces of Louis XV. and Marie Antoinette, reproduced in photogravure from exceedingly rare and well-executed contemporary engravings, and the impression of the book is strictly limited to 250 copies, each numbered. The book is choicely printed on fine paper, and bound in blue cloth extra, with appropriate gilt cover design. Price, to subscribers only, Two Guineas net.

Self-Seekers. A Novel by ANDRE

RAFFALOVICH. Crown 8vo. Price 4s. net.

The Fool and his Heart ; being the

plainly told story of Basil Thimm. A Novel by F. NORREYS CONNELL. Crown 8vo. Price 4s. 6d. net.

Hidden Witchery. Stories by NIGEL

TOURNEUR. Illustrated by Will Mein. Crown 8vo. Price 4s. net.

Unparalleled Patty : A Tale of

Life in London. By THOMAS GRAY. Crown 8vo. Price 3s. 6d. net.

Aurora la Cujiñi. A Realistic Sketch

in Seville. By R. B. CUNNINGHAME GRAHAM. With a Frontispiece. Imperial 16mo. Price 5s. net.

Literary London. Sketches by W. P.

RYAN. Large post 8vo.

[*Out of print.*

Alone. A Novel by Φ.

Crown 8vo. Price 6s. net.

Last Links with Byron, Shelley, and
Keats. By WM. GRAHAM. Large post 8vo. Price 6s. net.

A Chaplet of Love Poems. By
ETHEL M. DE FONBLANQUE (Mrs Arthur Harter). Large post 8vo. Price 5s. net.

[Ready in December 1898.

Verses at Sunset. By Mrs E. F.
CUNLIFFE. Large post 8vo. Price 5s. net.

London Fairy Tales. By A. D.
LEWIS. Illustrated by the Artist. Foolscap 4to. Price 4s. net.

[Ready in January 1899.

Arabesques. Impressions of Travel
by CYPRIAN COPE. Demy 8vo. Price 14s. net.

[Ready in January 1899.

Odd Issues. Stories by S. S.
SPRIGGE. Crown 8vo. Price 4s. net.

[Ready in January 1899.

Circulars of any of the above Books will be sent on application to

LEONARD SMITHERS & CO.
5 OLD BOND STREET, LONDON, W.

www.ingramcontent.com/pod-product-compliance
Lightning Source LLC
Chambersburg PA
CBHW030904050726
47500CB00009B/1011